Madison K.

NINA KAPLAN

ISBN: 1463749856

ISBN 13: 9781463749859

Library of Congress Control Number: 2011912951
CreateSpace, North Charleston, SC

*For my son Mason and my daughter Madison,
who inspire me every day of my life.
For my husband Michael, whom I love and who
always believes in me, and for my BFF Lisa.
My life is good because of all of you.*

Chapter 1

IT IS A BEAUTIFUL SATURDAY morning in the relaxed suburbs of Bucks County, Pennsylvania. Madison Kensington has lived in the same house her entire life. Her home is a typical middle class single, surrounded by the manufactured developments of the day. Madison is a passionate young girl, who is inspired by all that she experiences. She loves life and the extraordinary details of her visual world. She consumes and articulates a very specific vision that is her own. In many ways she is just a typical teenage girl, living in a typical suburban neighborhood, searching for a voice for her passions and inspirations.

But there is something about Madison that transcends the usual. She has a driving sense of responsibility and enthusiasm unlike most girls her age. She has a clear artistic dream that she wants to convey to women everywhere. She truly believes that genuine knowledge, integrity, and creativity are the most significant aspects of life experience and she always strives to be better. She is as flawed as she is fabulous, and through her passions and insecurities, she aims to find integrity within her world. Art and the art of beauty embody the world of Madison K.

Today is June 16, a very significant day in the young life of Madison K. She is sound asleep in dream mode. The sun is just slightly peeking through her window. She is adorned in her very hot-pink sleep mask, and her funky mismatched pajamas, and her face is covered with her favorite mint julep facial mask. Madison tends to break out on her nose and is OCD when it comes to fighting pimples. She is personified by her eclectic collections of vintage fabrics, clothing, and various items of inspiration that she has been accumulating since she was a little girl. Her unique environment is an artistic history of her young life as she surrounds herself with flea market finds and thrift store bargains. Because of Madison's eloquent placement of things they take on a strange modernity that is very much unique to her. Madison has the ability to take something old and make it new and relevant. She has been shopping and collecting with her mom since she was five years old and has a history and life experience way beyond her eighteen years.

Madison is in a deep sleep dreaming of her big day. Her best friend, a white Pomeranian, named Zsa Zsa, is lying next to her in her favorite position. She is on her back with all four paws in the air, and she too, is sound asleep. Madison acquired her BFF when Mrs. Brickman, the somewhat eccentric old lady next door, could no longer care for her dog. Madison enjoyed quite a deep relationship with Mrs. Brickman, and she made sure to check in on her daily. She has known Zsa Zsa since she was a pup and loved the stories Mrs. Brickman associated with naming her dog. She would talk joyfully of Princess Zsa Zsa and speak of old Hollywood on a daily basis. Madison loved

Mrs. Brickman's stories and didn't even mind their repetition. Last year when Mrs. Brickman became critically ill, she only wanted Madison to care for her Zsa Zsa. Sadly, Mrs. Brickman soon passed away, and since then, Madison has maintained full custody.

Madison looks peaceful with a jovial smile on her face. Her lips begin to move to her favorite Katy Perry song as her fabulous and funky alarm clock sings, "Baby You're a Firework." Madison jumps up, Zsa Zsa starts barking, and the mayhem begins. She immediately goes into OCD mode. Today is graduation, and she has everything to do: hair, makeup, nails!

OMG what to do first? Madison always has an articulate and stylized look. She is a spirited artist and loves to present different looks for different events. It is very important to Madison to speak through her choices. After all, an artist must express herself through her presentation. It is a matter of social humanity: she is sure of that! Madison says what she means and she means what she says, verbally and visually.

Madison articulates the art of makeup, fashion, and beauty in her own unique way. She experiments with color, texture, and style as often as possible. Her ideas are unconventional and she breaks many of the so-called rules of beauty. She often thinks about her mom's stories of how she was taught makeup application by the department store clerks. They would say that only certain colors were for certain people. Madison vehemently disagrees and is sure that if done properly, color can work to express each woman's distinctive qualities. Simply put, Madison has rewritten the rules, and she applies them to both beauty and fashion.

She is sure that how a woman looks and the message that they want to convey should be unique, and that communication and self-esteem are always the goal. But even more important to Madison is building the individual.

She takes her mission seriously and knows every trick, and every product, and loves all the fun and fuss that goes with it. Her self-diagnosed OCD tends to make her obsess over every facet and thought, and she, at times, struggles not to over think.

She is a bundle of nervous excitement! First a bath, she decides. Madison loves the bathtub.

In fact, she does her best and most creative thinking there. Her black vintage claw foot tub, which she begged her mother to drag home from one of their many flea market adventures, is adorned perfectly to her liking. She spent countless hours refinishing this baby and it is one of her favorite treasures. Details inspire her. She loves ornate and ornamented architecture. Old carvings, baroque furniture, and crystal lampshades are just some of Madison's collections. She refers to these things as "curls, swirls, and pearls" and loves the churchlike qualities and handmade details. The history intrigues her young mind, and she often wonders about the people who actually made the things she cherishes. She is truly in awe of their talents.

There are pictures everywhere of her friends and family. They, too, are adorned in vintage frames, which Madison has meticulously hand detailed. She spends countless hours recreating her flea market finds. She paints, patterns, and jewels almost all of her favorite possessions. She has a tasteful flair, a steady hand, and uniquely redesigns her things beautifully to her liking.

Scents are also part of Madison's obsessions. She often jokes about her bloodhound abilities. She is sure that she can actually identify almost every botanical or fragranced ingredient known to humankind. She takes pride in her gifted nose and gives credit to her mother's talent for gardening. Madison's mom is an avid gardener and has managed to grow, what Madison refers to as the Jungles of Nicaragua, in her backyard. She is sure that there is no species her mom hasn't uncovered. Madison enjoys an occasional walk through the lovely botanicals and researches the many fragrant aromas that tickle her nose.

What could be better than a fragrant bath filled with her favorite essential oils and of course bubbles? That will surely wake up the senses and get her neurons moving.

Zsa Zsa is now awake and alert. She follows Madison's every move and plants herself on the fabulously fringed and bejeweled ottoman placed strategically next to the tub. She lies there in a sea of bubbles practicing her interview speech. After graduation, she has an interview for a coveted internship with Faction, one of the largest cosmetic companies in the world, and this internship comes with pay. Madison really wants this opportunity and really needs the funding. She is already enrolled in Hunter College, and this internship will give her the resources and the experience she needs to succeed. Through Madison's relentless blogging, and creation of *Shimmer Magazine*, she has managed to catch the eye of the CEO. He is interested in all that she has achieved. She has been writing it online since she was twelve years old and is proud of her accomplishment. She has designed and written every last detail, and she has evolved her thoughts into a five page online magazine, along with a weekly blog, "Madison's Favorites."

Madison has always expressed her love and knowledge of the beauty industry and has the pulse of newness right on her fingertips. She is a product junkie and spends endless hours researching and trying new things. Through her own shopping experiences, Madison began to realize at a very young age that the market was flooded with millions of products. Some of these products were not so good, while others that received poor endorsements were fabulous! She found this to be a disturbing trend and began questioning the dubious ratings given. So, she continued to research as much as possible and was convinced that in many cases, the reviews were so off that the editors could not have been testing these products. She set out to bring her own love of beauty, *with integrity,* to the public. With this mission, she found her passion and hasn't looked back since.

Madison always does the hard work. She spends countless hours researching products, ingredients, and her favorite packaging. She is, of course, a sucker for beautiful packaging. While she loves a sugar coating, she must find the heart and soul of each and every product. She even recruits her mom and her friends to try things, and asks them to give her feedback. At times the work can be quite exhausting and overwhelming. This is a challenge that Madison takes seriously, as she really wants to give the best information that she can.

People have started to take notice of Madison's unique skills. Madison was, and still is, the beauty guru for her friends and family, and it has been spreading throughout the community that she is approaching her product reviews with truth, honesty, and fun.

As she lies in the fragrant tub, she continues to practice for her interview.

"Hello. Uh, hi so-meet, uh, so nice to meet you. I have been writing and designing my own magazine, uh"

"Ugh, I need to be more fluid. I need to be more confident."

Madison looks at Zsa.

"Do I sound tentative?"

She waits for Zsa Zsa to give her a lick, a head nod, or some positive sign. Madison has to work harder than most at her verbal presentations, as she has always been dyslexic. Diagnosed with a left-brain processing disorder in sixth grade, she never let the label stop her from keeping up. She just worked through it like anyone else would. But many times her words get mixed up. Because she wants to be a great writer, she writes and rewrites excessively, checking and rechecking her words. It has taken a lot of hard work and perseverance for her to become the writer that she is today. She tries not to take herself too seriously, but she is oh so passionate.

She still has many oops moments and tangled sentences that can sometimes get her into quite a mess. She is grateful for the LOL acronym, so that when she does commit a tiny error, she is able to laugh at herself along with her fans. Her keen sense of humor has helped her get through even the most embarrassing moments.

Zsa Zsa listens to her intently and gives her the signature head tilt. She is sure that her baby understands her, and that she is truly her best critic.

"Okay Zsa, here I go again. Hello, my name is Madison K. I," She bursts out laughing and dunks herself completely under the water. She pops up with her face full of bubbles and starts laughing uncontrollably.

"Oh my god, Zsa! I am so nervous, I hope I don't mess this up, I want this so bad! Faction Cosmetics is the biggest. They make so many of the products I love. It's my dream job."

She laughs again and Zsa Zsa is now up on her feet and begins to lick all the bubbles off of Madison's face. Madison grabs her, schnoogles her nose, and looks her right in the eyes. FYI, "schnoogling" is one of Madison's many made-up words, meaning something a bit more than regular snuggling.

"What would I do without you Zsa?"

Madison then pulls her pup right up into her face, gives her lots of kisses, and then dunks Zsa Zsa and herself in the water. She pops up quickly, gives Zsa Zsa another hug, and then wraps herself and her baby in a fabulous fluffy hot-pink bath towel. She puts her down and Zsa Zsa shakes off the excess bubbles, completely re-soaking Madison. She snarls playfully at her dog, and grabs another towel. As she is drying herself off her phone starts singing a familiar song, "She's a Maniac." Madison shakes out her hair, quickly wraps it in a towel and dashes to the bedroom. Zsa Zsa follows quickly behind, jumps up on her bed and circles a beautiful array of handmade pillows. She digs the perfect spot and plops herself down. Madison quickly picks up the phone, mid song.

"Yes my maniac girlfriend? What's up?" On the other end is Jade Skillman. Jade is one of Madison's best friends. They met in preschool, and even when they were separated in high school, they, along with their other BFF Kia, remained best friends.

Jade is quite different from Madison, yet their friendship is strengthened by a core of integrity. Their passions can be endlessly impossible and pretty exhausting. Jade's passions lie in the fashion industry, and she is a dark brooding artist, who at times, hates Madison's squeaky clean good girl attitude. Many times Jade, not purposely, brings Madison down with her cynical nature. She considers herself a realist, while she is sure that Madison is an idealist.

Jade was made for the fashion industry. She is very tall, enviably thin, and she too is an artsy girl. Jade is biracial and is blessed with her Japanese mom's very angular features and her Irish dad's extraordinary physique. She is often approached to model but has no interest. She is confident that she will be a successful fashion designer. Jade has a razor sharp edge, and at times, she can be extremely difficult. Jade and Madison have been best friends since they were five, and though they have strong differences, they truly love and respect each other. While Jade is tough on the outside, her heart is that of a dedicated friend and a good human being. Madison is sure of this.

"So are you ready"? Jade asks. Madison takes a quick look in the mirror.

"Ugh! I have such dark circles under my eyes and I have this huge pimple on my nose. Just another beauty trauma for the day."

"Just another day in the life of Madison K.," says Jade while laughing and rolling her eyes. "You are such a drama queen. You always look perfect, and besides, you're like fricken' Michelangelo with makeup." They both laugh, as they know this to be true.

"Today is your day girl," says Jade. "You need to get this right because after you graduate, you need to secure that internship so we can finish our plan as scheduled." The girls, Madison, Jade, and Kia, made a pact when they were twelve that after they graduated they were going to New York to pursue their dreams. Jade and Kia had their graduation from a prestigious private school last week, and now they are anxiously awaiting for their BFF to get her diploma so that they can move forward with their plans.

The girls often discussed what they wanted to be when they became adults. Madison is the beauty writer and entrepreneur, Jade is the fashion designer, and Kia, is going to be a legal hotshot and even has aspirations in politics. Jade just secured an amazing internship with Bryce Martin, one of the top designers in New York, and has also secured a spot at the coveted Fashion Institute of Technology. Kia has been accepted to NYU, and now if Madison gets this gig, the plan will be complete.

The girls have all worked really hard for this day, and everyone is nervous and anxious as they wait for Madison's interview. First, Madison has to attend the graduation ceremony and then the interview. She has to walk at twelve, and then she has her scheduled interview at three. She tends to over think everything and has to make all attempts to calm herself down.

Jade always torturing Madison, tells her "Now, no pressure Mads, just don't mess this up. Keep your words straight and give em all you got. You got this! You are great at what you do. Just breathe!"

Madison responds anxiously as usual. "Oh my god, I am freaking out!"

"Like I said, just breathe!" says Jade. She is used to the drama that is Madison K. "They will love you. Everybody does," she says with the customary sarcasm that by now Madison is used to, and Madison can just imagine Jade's infamous eye roll.

Jade does this with true affection, as she really does have great respect for her best friend.

"K, J" Madison responds sharply "I got to go. I have to get ready. You and Kia are coming today, aren't you?"

"Really? You are kidding. You just sat in the pouring rain to watch us get our diplomas and we won't miss our girl getting her hard earned diploma. Oh, and, Mads…try not to trip on stage," Jade jokes.

"Thanks J, as if I am not nervous enough."

Jade reminds Madison that she tends to get so impassioned in her thoughts, that, well frankly, she can be a real klutz.

"That's what we love about you Mads. You always look great, but are predictably available for a laugh or two."

Jade can't help herself. Her constant needling gets the best of everyone. She tends to verbalize the negative. Madison does not like the negative tone that Jade sometimes brings to the table, and this is where the girls part ways. Mads may be kind and fun, but she too has a sharp tongue and razor quickness. These two BFFs go toe-to-toe often and at times their banter is quite intense. Madison handles Jade's cynicism well, and that keeps Jade in check.

"Gotcha, thanks for the confidence booster." They both laugh.

"Hey I really do have to go. I am already running late. I will be looking for you guys in the crowd." Madison hangs up and quickly continues her pursuit to beauty.

Ah, what to wear? She carefully scans her very disorganized and colorful closet. It is full of vintage and contemporary looks. She brings her flea market and second hand finds to Jade who possesses expert sewing ability, and together they recreate fabulous looks for Madison to wear. Madison's closet is bright and beautiful and very pink! Today she finds the perfect little pink dress. Not too bright, but not too bland.

She holds it up in the mirror and then looks for her best critic. Zsa Zsa…

"Well, what do you think?" She turns around and Zsa Zsa is sound asleep as the bath really tired her out. Madison giggles and decides for herself that Zsa Zsa will approve. She sprays some detangler in her hair and begins to blow-dry. Her mom knocks on her door and reminds her that the time is running short. She looks at the clock and realizes her mom is right, as always! She has got to hurry. She rummages through her accessories, shoes, earrings, and belts. No belt, she decides. Madison always seems to be running late. No matter how much she tries to plan her day, it seems that the time just gets away from her. Thank god, she has her makeup down to a science: primer, foundation, and definitely a bit of concealer. Her dark circles drive her insane. Then she finishes her look with a little extra bronzer, as she can't look too pale. *It might give her nerves away,* she thinks.

With clothing scattered and a trail of makeup, Madison is dressed and ready to go. She flies down the steps and heads for the door. She hands Zsa to her mom, making her promise to bring her, and off she goes. Her mom stops her abruptly.

"I just want to tell you how proud I am of you and how much I love you. You know, your dad would be so proud if he could see you today."

Madison's dad died of cancer when she was eleven. She misses him every day, but never feels sorry for herself. Her mom reminds her often of the wonderful traits she inherited from her dad. Madison reminds her mom that she has the most supportive and annoying mom on the planet. She feels lucky and grateful to have her mom but thinks of her dad often and wishes he could be here today. She feels a well of tears coming and scolds her mom for the possibility of messing up her makeup. Her mom reassures her that everyone knows that Madison's make-up does not move. They laugh, and hug, and Madison hits the ground running.

She is, of course, running late. By the time she gets to the stadium there is just about five minutes before they start. Madison slips on her graduation gown, perfectly pins on her graduation cap and hurries toward the crowd. She looks around at the large class of her fellow graduates, and she feels a sense of pride. She did it. It wasn't easy, and at times it was quite trying especially with her dyslexia. Not only did Madison graduate with a 3.5, but she wrote many articles for the school paper and even had a piece published in *Lucky Magazine*. She is proud of herself.

"Well here we go!" she says out loud. She lines up and starts to walk, and scans the crowd looking for her girls. Madison figures they should be easy to find. She just has to look for the tallest, thinnest girl dressed in long sleeves and all black, in the middle of June. Jade is never hard to find. Madison laughs to herself as she spots her. Never to disappoint, Jade is a standout in the sea of soft hues. She waves to her friends, and they shout back.

"We love you Madison!"

Madison is busy looking back and gets a bit distracted, and as she gets closer, she begins thinking more about her interview.

"Madison Kensington" is spoken at the podium. The girl behind her politely nudges her.

"That's you."

Madison replies, "Uh, oh thanks," and she refocuses to hear her name. She speeds up her pace, stands tall, and walks with pride. Madison accepts her diploma, shakes the principal's hand, and quickly moves off the stage. She glances up into the crowd and hears her girls yelling.

"Yay, Mads, you got it!"

Madison looks up, waves, and then, a bit embarrassed, scurries to her seat. Again her mind is elsewhere, and the next thing she hears is the crowd roar, and all the graduation caps fly up in the air. Madison has bobby pinned her cap firmly and perfectly. She forgot about the cap toss, and when she grabs it, it is stuck firmly to her head. She looks around and blushes and then quickly takes out the bobby pins, and in perfect Madison K. style, tosses her cap a good one minute after the crowd. Madison K. has graduated!

Her girls, family, and Zsa Zsa come down to the field and hug and congratulate her, and rag on her about her brief missteps. Her girlfriends surround her.

"We're so proud of you."

"You did great."

"Yeah," Jade reminds her, "I loved the part where your cap was stuck to your head."

"Thanks Jade I know I can always count on you for the positive."

"I speak with true affection. That moment really took the torture out of watching the event." Jade quips back.

"You know the expected unexpected, signature Madison K." Kia shoots a look toward Jade and pulls Madison aside.

"Don't listen to Jade," says Kia. "She just can't help herself. We really are so proud of you; you are beautiful, smart, and talented. You look gorgeous."

"Thanks K you're the… oh, god! "

Madison nervously runs her fingers through her hair.

"How's my hair? Can you see my circles? Uh am I wrinkled?" She laughs. "My dress, I mean….did I look okay?"

"Stop! You're perfect!" says Kia. She affectionately puts her arm around Madison, and says, "You really are a nut." They all look at each other and laugh.

Chapter 2

MADISON K. IS NOW A high school graduate, and she has one hour until her big interview. The CEO of Faction Cosmetics has agreed to interview her nearby at a local Westin. Madison has fifteen minutes, and then she must be on her way. She hangs out with her friends and family, and then goes home to change into her perfect interview outfit. She has spent hours coordinating this look. Madison finally decided on a fabulous black skirt (not too short of course) a pink matte jersey tank, and the most adorable vintage black-and-white nubby Jackie O style jacket. She and Jade found it at a flea market and remade it beautifully.

Madison has been planning this outfit for quite some time, and she is sure that it is right for the occasion.

She quickly runs in the house and slips into her clothes, touches up her makeup, and jumps back into the car. She still has a fifteen-minute ride to the Westin, and lateness is not an option. She cranks up the radio and allows her favorite tunes to calm her nerves. She sings her songs loudly and passionately. Maybe a bit off tune, but singing always works to clear her mind. Madison is ready for her interview.

She pulls up to the Westin and notices that there must be some major event going on as she has to park very far from the entrance. The parking lot is completely full, and the valet is just too busy for her to take a chance on being late. Madison is not the best of drivers and especially has difficulty parallel parking. She drives way over to the back end of the lot and luckily finds a spot. Out of the corner of her eye she sees a parade of some very fancy cars. *Must be a big deal person having that event,* Madison thinks to herself. She is, for once, on time and even has five minutes to spare.

Her meeting is in the Brigade Room on the second floor. She checks in at the front desk and heads up the elevator. The Brigade Room is right off the elevator, and Madison walks inside to a very grand, but very empty room. She is the first to arrive. She is relieved and wants to take a few moments to gather her thoughts. She sits down and waits. Madison looks around at the large intimidating room. She's never been to the Westin before. It reminds her of the Hilton where Kia had her sweet sixteen party. Very fancy, but somehow lacking the boutique quality that she loves. She is sure that she could decorate it a bit better and bring some much-needed warmth to the room. Beautiful, but a bit staid for her. Madison just can't help herself.

Just as she is redecorating in her mind, a tall gentleman enters the room. Madison quickly rises. He reaches out to her hand.

"Madison?"

She is a bit intimidated and quickly examines him. He is perfectly suited and coiffed, with every hair in place. He has steely eyes, grayed temples, and perfectly polished shoes. He is wearing a gorgeous Italian suit.

This guy must be the real deal, Madison thinks. Madison straightens her posture and receives him.

"Mr. Grayson? It's so nice to meet you." Madison says confidently.

"Nice to meet you too Madison," he replies. "Congratulations on your graduation. I am sorry that our interview had to be today, but my schedule has been quite difficult."

Leonard Grayson speaks with what Madison refers to as an elitist mentality, and while he is nothing but polite, he seems cold.

"Well, shall we sit down?" Madison nods, and they both sit down. Madison feels her stride and starts to express her passion.

"First I want to say that I am so excited with the prospect of interning for your company and for the opportunity to publish my magazine. I can't tell you how exciting that is to me."

"Your accomplishments are enviable, Madison. I must say you have done a tremendous job with your magazine. I have read it many times and am very impressed with your drive. I am a man who knows when something is good and I think *Shimmer Magazine* has great potential. I have a contract with me, and we would like to offer you a real chance to publish."

Madison is floored that he has barely even spoken to her, and here is an offer on the table. She is confused and a bit taken back. Her mind starts to race and she slows down the conversation. She states that she would like to read the agreement and that she is flattered at the generous nature of the opportunity. She smiles awkwardly, but just doesn't trust the man sitting across from her. Something in her gut feels wrong. She tells him that she would like to know more about the prospect. Mr. Grayson seems a bit impatient and almost annoyed that Madison would like the opportunity to read the agreement or even question him at all.

She glances down at the overwhelming document and three words stand out as alarming. *Ownership of Shimmer.* It suddenly dawns on her. They did not want her. They want her magazine and her readership. At least that's what it seems like. Madison's eyes start to fill up, and she excuses herself from the room. She tells Mr. Grayson that she needs to go to the restroom. Madison runs down the hallway to the restroom and shuts the door behind her. As she starts to move toward the stall, she slams right into an older, attractive, and very well dressed woman. Everything flies into the air, Madison's bag, the woman's bag, and, oh god, she knocks the woman right to the floor.

"Oh my god" Madison cries. "Let me help you. I am sooo sorry. I didn't even see....oh god, I am so, so sorry."

The woman quickly composes herself. "I am all right!" she says firmly. Madison can't help fixating on her beautifully applied makeup. Maybe she is around forty-five years old, Madison guesses. Still crying, Madison continues picking up all the woman's things off the floor and quickly gets distracted by the lovely contents of the woman's purse. With tears streaming down her face, she sees a familiar compact.

"Oh, I love that! I have the pink one. It is such a great bronzer, and such a pretty compact. Don't you think?" Madison remarks.

The woman is a bit stunned and continues to compose herself. She signals Madison to hand over her things and then walks towards the mirror. Madison again continues to apologize as she follows the woman to the mirror.

"My god I can't tell you how sorry I am, I was just so upset. I mean, why are people like this? Why do they say one thing and mean another?" Madison glances into the mirror. "Oh god! Look at me! I'm a complete mess, and on top of everything, I clearly can't sign a contract like that with Faction. What a jerk," she huffs under her breath.

The woman swings her head around and is clearly interested in what Madison is saying. "Faction?" she asks with a bit of scorn. Still fixing her face and gathering herself in the mirror she turns to Madison and introduces herself.

She extends her hand and says, "Hello I am Nina Hagen. You seem to have a great eye for cosmetics. I can't say much for your entrance, but you can definitely recognize the good stuff." She looks at Madison and actually feels bad as she sees that she is visibly shaken. "Are you okay?" Nina asks.

Madison starts babbling about the interview, about the woman's fabulous choice of cosmetics, and about the way that she believes Mr. Grayson, might be trying to steal her idea.

"Ah" Nina says, making the connection. What Madison is unaware of is that Nina Hagen, at one time, worked for Leonard Grayson, and the fact that they are both at the Westin today, may just be a stroke of luck for Madison. Nina Hagen and Leonard Grayson are both attending Lauren Laden's wedding. Faction Cosmetics belongs to her father. It seems her fiancé is from Bucks County, and this is the event that Madison saw as she was coming in. Nina makes the connection and comforts Madison.

"Well young lady it is no easy feat to land an interview with Leonard Grayson. You must have something he really wants."

"You know him? She says, sniffling.

"Know him!" Nina laughs. "I worked with him for ten years."

"He wanted me to sign over my magazine. I think, maybe I was reading it wrong. Oh god, now what am I going to do? I just graduated today, and over the phone he seemed so nice, but when I looked at the contract, I mean I really didn't get a chance to look at it, but I think he just wanted control of my magazine. I mean I know I am young, and I know I have a lot to learn, but I have been writing this magazine since I was twelve, and I was so excited that I got this interview, and I know that I am a nobody, but I have worked so hard, and I just thought that, I mean, oh god, I don't even know you. First I almost kill you and now I am blubbering all of my issues at you. I am such an idiot. God, I am a mess."

She begins to compose herself. "Wait, what did you say? Did you say that you know him? You did say that, didn't you? Ugh, what does it matter, I really messed this up."

Madison now realizes that she has little or no chance of getting this internship, and she may have blown a real chance to publish her magazine.

She now focuses on Nina who comforts her and tells her that Leonard Grayson has a great eye for talent, and that yes, he is a snake, but he knows when something is good. She also congratulates Madison on her keen instincts and assures her that there will be more opportunities for her. She is quite taken with Madison and what Madison also does not know is that Nina has just started her own beauty concept and she is looking for an assistant, a writer, and a blogger.

Nina continues to chat with Madison and assures her that if Leonard Grayson is after her ideas they must be good ones.

"That's what he does. He scours the media for young talent and then he tries to cultivate and steal their ideas. I assure you I know. He did it to me. I worked for him for 10 years. He used me and you know what? I used him right back. Now I won't say that that is always the way to go, but one learns from one's mistakes."

Nina laughs. "Don't worry about your behavior; you have a good nose for the untrustworthy. Watch out for Leonard Grayson! If I were you, I would walk right back in there and stand your ground. You must be very good at what you do to have gotten his attention. Just do not sign anything without a lawyer looking it over."

Madison is dazed. "I just graduated today, and I guess I am naïve, but I thought that I was getting this great situation, and I was going to have an opportunity to build my magazine and work in the industry. I guess I am just inexperienced. I just…I didn't,"

Nina extends her hand to Madison and gives her a business card. "If things don't work out with Faction, give me a call. I am on my own now, and I am building an amazing concept. You might be interested. I would like to see your work."

Madison is now completely drained and realizes that she has left Mr. Grayson for more than fifteen minutes. She quickly thanks Nina for speaking to her and again profusely apologizes for knocking her down. She quietly slips out the door, and she re-enters the Brigade Room, but Mr. Grayson is gone. There is a note on the table.

ᏔᎥᎦ ᏔᎥᎦ ᏔᎥᎦ

Madison,

Sorry I could not wait. I was late for another meeting. I will be in touch.

Fondly,
Leonard Grayson.

ᏔᎥᎦ ᏔᎥᎦ ᏔᎥᎦ

Madison grabs the closest chair and slinks down into it and begins to sob. She is angry with herself, as she knows that her emotions can get the best of her. She mentally beats herself up and wonders how she is going to tell the girls that she has failed. She sits there in silence. Her fists are clenched, and she looks down at the card she has been holding on to since she left the restroom.

It says, BLC BEAUTY, with the most fabulous logo. Underneath, it says www.beautylandcouture. com, New York, New York Nina Hagen 212 475 8267. *Beauty? New York?* Madison rethinks the last forty-five minutes.

Well my mother always told me that when one door closes, another one opens. I think that door is definitely closed. Maybe I can turn this into something positive, she thinks to herself.

She sits for a few more minutes, and then she heads out. She again notices the barrage of beautiful cars in the lot.

Wow that must be some event, she thinks to herself.

Chapter 3

NINA RETURNS TO HER HOTEL room at the Westin, opens up her laptop and Googles Madison K. She also takes out her notebook and begins her search. She finds a blog, a Facebook page, and *Shimmer Magazine*. This has Nina's attention. She studies the unusual layout and the artistic flair. She reads a few of the entries and likes what she sees. This may be just the girl she is looking for. Nina is building her own beauty concept and likes many of the ideas that Madison has executed. She wonders if they may be able to help each other. She sees real promise in what Madison is doing and would like to speak to her further.

Nina has worked in the beauty industry for the last twenty years. After ten years with Grayson, she knew it was time to go out on her own. She is smart, articulate, and creative. She is also savvy and knows what it takes to succeed in the current market. She has designed a very new idea for beauty, and with the funds she has just secured, Nina Hagen is armed and ready. She is a shrewd businesswoman, but unlike Leonard Grayson, she has a heart. Nina continues to read, while taking notes and making lists. She peeks at the time on her computer and realizes that she must get ready for the wedding. She closes her laptop and heads for the bathroom. It's time to get ready for the wedding of the year.

Madison is back in her car, and she starts thinking. She has a tendency to verbalize her thoughts out loud. Sometimes she wishes she had a filter and sometimes she definitely needs one. And on this quiet ride home she searches for answers.

"Okay, this was not your best performance," she says out loud. "Just learn, think, and for god's sake stop being so darn emotional. You're smart, you're articulate and you are good at what you do. Just believe in yourself. It will all work out. Believe!"

"Hey, congratulations Madison. You should be very proud of yourself. You are a......"

Muffled music interrupts Madison's self help talk. She reaches into her glove compartment, where she left her cell phone. It is singing another familiar song. She decides not to answer her mom's call. She opens the sunroof and blasts the radio. She begins to sing her heart out. Belting out 80s tunes always helps her feel better. She will tackle this new development tomorrow. Right now there are a ton of graduation parties calling her name, and she needs to let loose and have some fun. She thinks about how she will break the news to her family and her girls. *Well it's not done yet,* she thinks. She can still send out her resume, and she can call Nina. *Maybe it was meant to be.* Hey she still has her magazine, and her readership. Things will look better tomorrow.

The one thing that Madison has is optimism. Her manic ADD and OCD make her nutty before a situation, but after the craziness is over, she is always able to calm herself down and become more rational. It's the nerves that get her every time.

She pulls into the driveway, and the house looks dark. This is good news. She can take some time alone and reflect until she is bombarded with questions. She opens the door and turns on the lights.

"Surprise!" everyone yells at once. Her girls, her mom, her entire family are there. Madison instantly turns to Jell-O. They are all over her. She quickly composes herself and lovingly receives her friends and family.

Jade goes first. "So, my girl, how was the interview? Are you in?"

Madison responds, "I think … I uh…" It is no use. Madison is a terrible liar, and from the look on her face, they all know that the interview definitely did not go well. Even Jade pulls back on her attitude and just gives Madison what she needs.

"You know what Mads? They don't deserve you. You will show them. We all know what you can do, and they will too."

Madison continues to tell her entire story, and then the crowd starts to disburse and enjoy the celebration. She moves through the crowded entranceway and notices the beautiful decorations and the way her mom created everything she loves. The table is set with pretty desserts, a beautiful array of all the vintage glassware, and linens that they have collected together. Her mom is a true inspiration to her, and she is so grateful to have her. She pulls her mom aside and thanks her. She reminds her that without her she wouldn't be the person that she is.

Madison's mom is quiet in a way that Madison is not. She is outwardly calm and internally strong. She knows that Madison has many of her dad's qualities, and she is quick to remind her again how much he loved her. She strokes her hand through Madison's hair and gives her the look that her daughter needs, and just with that, Madison is calmed.

The guest of honor continues graciously greeting all of her friends and family. After about twenty minutes of polite behavior, she makes her way to her room. She just needs five minutes with Zsa Zsa and a quick makeup redo and definitely some air. She needs to compose her thoughts. Madison has had to grow up a bit today. She learned a big lesson in life, and she is sure that more opportunities as well as more rejection will come. She falls back on her bed and takes a deep breath. "Live to fight another day." She says out loud. Her dad always told her that.

Back in OCD mode, Madison is sitting in front of the makeup mirror reapplying her eye makeup. *What a mess* she thinks. Zsa Zsa is there by her side, sensing that Madison just needs her to be quiet. She watches a true artist at work. Kia, and Jade knock on the door. They go all serious on Madison, and this just makes her crazy.

Kia says, "We just wanted you to know…"

Madison cuts her right off. "I know. You guys are the best friends anyone could ever ask for. Really, I am so okay. I know what you guys want to say, and I appreciate it. But, I am completely all right. In fact I am good, really good. Tomorrow is another day, and besides" a huge smile comes over Madison's entire face. "Did you see the amazing cake down there?"

They all laugh. Madison and Kia always have to watch what they eat, while Jade, could eat 24/7 and never gain an ounce. Madison decides that this is definitely a cake moment, and she and Kia waste no time getting downstairs. Special occasions and cake always go together.

The girls party and enjoy the evening. They stay at Madison's house for a few hours and then they stop in to a few more parties. After many hours of celebrating, Madison is definitely ready to go home. She leaves the girls to continue their party hopping and heads home. When she gets to her front door, she sees a large black box with a beautiful hot pink bow on it. Just by the look of the box, she is sure that it must be for her. She sees a card that says Madison. She opens the box, and thirteen hot-pink roses lie inside. Each rose is carefully manicured and has a tube of water attached to it. She opens the card and it reads.

So sorry I couldn't be with you today. I put in an extra rose for good luck.
Collin

With all the fuss and all the insanity of the day, Madison realized that Collin her one time boyfriend and now very good friend was not at her party. He graduated last year and has been attending Columbia University in New York City. He left for a summer internship in Tunisia two weeks ago, and Madison completely forgot about Collin. Collin, however, did not forget about Madison. He was her good friend all through middle school. He was always a bit of a geek with a fabulous sense of humor and he was, and still is, wickedly brilliant.

Collin had a huge crush on Madison in high school, and they even dated briefly in her junior year. Madison went to Collin's senior prom, and later, they both decided that they were better as friends. They even made a pact that if neither of them found the perfect significant other by the time that they were thirty, they would revisit their relationship. Madison smiles from this memory and thinks fondly of Collin. He was always there for her and he was so genuine. She could always just be herself around him.

Wow that was so sweet, and how did you get these here? My god you are in Tunisia. Impressive, she thinks. *You always were the smartest guy in the room.*

Madison picks up the box and smells the fragrant flowers. So beautiful, she laughs to herself, and under her breath she says, "I won't break it to him that the thirteenth rose was a bust."

She actually laughs out loud, takes the flowers into the house and shuts the door. She is content that tomorrow is Sunday, and she has absolutely nowhere to be. She slips into her most comfortable Betsey pajamas, does a quick face wash, brushes her teeth and hits the pillow.

Madison awakens to a wet tongue on her face. Her eyes are so glued shut that she has trouble opening them. She knows that that means she did a bad makeup removal job last night, and she feels the mascara stuck to her eyelashes. Zsa Zsa is now on top of her, pawing at her and whining.

Madison is still very groggy as she says, "Zsa...stop! Okay, okay come on let's go out." Zsa Zsa begins to bark... "I'm coming I'm coming." Madison glances at the clock and she sees that she slept until eleven. This is late for her, as Madison is usually an early riser. No wonder

Zsa Zsa was relentless; this is a long time to hold it in. Madison drags herself out of her bed and slips on her favorite fuzzy slippers.

"Okay Zsa come on." She quickly takes her outside, and Zsa immediately pees. "Good girl" Madison praises her baby. Zsa Zsa is relieved both physically and emotionally as it is rare for her to have an accident. She loves the approval from Madison and soaks up the love.

Madison now takes a moment to notice the absolutely gorgeous, clear sunny day. This wakes her right up, and she decides that this will be a good day to start to get back to the pursuit of her dream. She will tackle her problems with spirit and intensity.

She thinks about her first interview experience and vows not to let that ever happen to her again. She takes a seat on the picnic table in her yard and gives Zsa Zsa some extra playtime. As she watches her dog playfully circling the trees, she ponders her next move. She knows that she must continue to pursue what she has started and what is burning inside of her. Today is just the beginning of a long, hard road.

Madison now calls Zsa Zsa and goes straight to her room to work. She figures that if she can get a decent job or an amazing internship, she can play musical money and work out the finances for New York. She has the next two months to work this out, and she is determined to do just that. She will be with her girls in September. She is back in OCD mode, as she sits at the computer and Googles BLC Beauty. She definitely wants to make contact with Nina Hagen. She liked her, and who knows, *maybe all of yesterday was meant to be.* She decides that beautylandcouture.com is an adorable website and wants to know more about BLC Beauty.

Wow, Nina Hagen has a Wikipedia page! How did I miss this? Madison wonders. She takes a ton of notes, especially about the website and the products chosen. She likes many of the products that Nina has on her site, and she loves the color and whimsy of the design. She wonders why she never heard of her. She realizes that there is much she does not know. She sees that Nina actually designed some of the packaging for Faction Cosmetics, and that Nina is no dummy, either. The woman got her BFA from

Tyler School of Art, and even attended Yale Graduate School of Fine Arts. She takes out the business card that Nina gave her and composes an e-mail.

❧ ❧ ❧

Dear Ms. Hagen

I am writing you, first, to sincerely apologize for knocking you down in the ladies room at the Westin. Thank you for being so understanding. I also wanted to say thanks for your kind words. They really helped me get through the rest of the day. I did not get a chance to speak to Mr. Grayson, as he was late for another meeting, but at this time, I know that I could never work for the kind of man I believe him to be.

I did some research, and I would love the opportunity to meet with you and discuss your concept. I am interested in how I might fit into your vision with my blog and magazine. I am attaching a few writing samples, along with the latest copy of Shimmer Magazine. I hope you enjoy reading them. Please contact me if you like what you read.

Kindest Regards,
Madison Kensington
267-644-6118

❦ ❦ ❦

She takes a breath and then hits send. Madison continues pounding the keys more determined than ever to find a good starting point. She will find a good job, and she will be with her girls in New York City. She sends out many more e-mails to many different venues of the beauty industry. She figures that someone must be looking for a hardworking, OCD, dyslexic writer like her. She laughs to herself.

Madison spends the next three hours working on her blog. She responds to numerous e-mails and product questions, and then she posts her latest experience. She writes:

I graduated yesterday. It was truly a magical day. I started off with a fragrant and most luxurious bath. I soaked my body in a moisturizing scoop of Choco-holic (of course). For those of you who have never experienced this fabulous bath ice cream, it is a must! One scoop will hydrate and nourish even the driest of skin. Oh, and it is also Zsa Zsa's favorite!

She tells her fans about dunking Zsa Zsa in the tub and all the fuss and fun of getting ready. She continues to share her special day with her fans, but is careful not to share the later events of the day. She has not told her fans about her interview or for that matter how she plans to move forward with her magazine and blog. She has about 10,000 followers, and to her, that is amazing.

She appreciates each and every one of her readers and makes sure to respond to any and all questions. She answers a few e-mails and then closes down her computer. Madison is starving. She realizes that she has not eaten a thing all day, and it is almost five. She reminds herself that she ate enough for the week yesterday, but her stomach reminds her that it does not agree.

The house is quiet. Her mom is at work - a typical Sunday. Madison's mom is a nurse and tends to have a crazy schedule. It seems that they are always missing each other. Madison looks at Zsa and thinks pizza! Zsa Zsa knows the look. One all natural Trader Joe's frozen pizza is left in the freezer. She looks at her baby and decides that this is fairly healthy and very delicious. She pops it into the oven, grabs a bottled water, and sets the table. She shares some pizza crust with Zsa Zsa and enjoys her dinner.

Chapter 4

NINA IS ALREADY ON HER way back to New York. She enjoys scenic route 263 in the heart of Bucks County. It is a gorgeous day, and she reflects on the evening behind her. She loved the bride's dress, but hated her headpiece. Nina is not one to mince words or teeter on an opinion. Her opinions are sure and finite. She has never been married and knows that it is just not the life for her, but she does love the art of the wedding and enjoys imagining the perfect wedding plan. All in all, she respected the bride's taste. The wedding was beautiful! *And thank god*, Nina thinks, *not another all white wedding,* this one was colorful and fun. For that she gives it a solid B+.

Nina also thinks about the young lady who knocked her over, but captivated her, in the restroom. She was intrigued by what she saw and what she read. *Madison K. I like her. I think a real interview is in order.* She continues to drive with the windows cracked and just relaxes. It is rare that she can do this, so a quiet ride is an absolute gift. She reaches into her bag for her Blackberry. Her phone is dead. That is so not like her. She must have had one glass of champagne too many. She is a bit annoyed at herself, as she plugs in her car charger and lets her phone recover.

Nina is almost back in New York City and smiles as she sees the detailed skyline. Every time she drives into New York she feels sadness when she does not see the twin towers. The skyline just feels wrong and Nina can't wait until they finish rebuilding. Nina was born and raised in Manhattan, and 9/11 is imbedded into her soul. She drives through the tunnel and sees her loft. Nina is relieved to be home. There is no city in the world like hers. That, she is sure of.

She parks her car and heads upstairs. Her apartment is a fabulous walk up on the outskirts of Chelsea. She likes that the stairs always force her to exercise, a chore that she truly detests. She tosses her bags to the side and glances at her now fully charged phone.

Nina scrolls her messages and deletes the spam and unfamiliar. *Ah!* She sees a familiar name madisonk1224@aol.com, and she is impressed. Ambition is something that Nina can relate to. She has been there and likes a girl who sees opportunity and takes the first step. She downloads Madison's sample writings and begins to read. She now sees the talent and passion that caught Leonard's eye. She continues reading and moves from her Blackberry to her laptop to format a reply.

✄ ✄ ✄

Dear Madison,

First let me say that in spite of our awkward collision, I did enjoy speaking with you the other day. I must say that I am very impressed with your drive and ambition. Your writing samples are quite good. I think you have a gift and great possibilities. Why don't we meet for coffee next week? I am attaching a personal statement about myself, and my concept. It might help you to understand who I am and where I am going.

Fondly,
Nina Hagen

❧   ❧   ❧

Today is Monday, and Madison has been a graduate for two days. In a way she feels a bit down. She is not used to having any real time on her hands and has a head full of racing thoughts. She wakes to a dark rainy day.

Zsa Zsa and rain are not a good combination. She hates going out in the rain, and it is a real chore for Madison to convince her otherwise. Madison signals to her to hurry and do her business. Zsa Zsa reluctantly scurries to the grass and goes and then dashes to the door. Madison is waiting with a fluffy towel for her baby. "Awe you're sooo wet." Madison says affectionately. She schnoogles her baby and wraps her lovingly and heads upstairs.

Madison opens her laptop, grabs her favorite extra comfy blanket and gets to work. Zsa Zsa circles and digs into the blanket, trying to wipe off the extra water soaked in her fur. Madison is hoping to find at least a few leads. Her eyes widen as she sees a familiar name. *Nina Hagen.* She swallows hard before reading it.

As she reads, she grabs Zsa Zsa and is elated. "She liked me Zsa," Madison says. A sense of excitement and anxiety come over her all at once. "Okay, I can do that. I can jump on the train and meet her anywhere she wants. Oh my god, please let this work out. I like Nina Hagen, I think.. Oh who knows?" Madison now realizes that there is an attachment in the e-mail.

What If (A Personal Statement)
What if we said what we meant and we meant what we said? What if we could make money based on the truth and a core of integrity? What if we sold products that we believed to be the best and then promoted them as such? A good idea and a creative

thought must come from a core of integrity or it is basically a lie.

Madison is completely captivated by Nina's words. She continues to read.

As an artist, I strive to represent truths based on facts and honesty. At the end of the day if we mean it, we will succeed.

Madison is engaged. This is a woman that she wants to get to know. She imagines what they could accomplish if they worked together. She now knows that this is meant to be. Nina Hagen is a unique and passionate individual. She also realizes that this is a great opportunity for her. This is where she needs to start her career. She continues reading, and Nina's inspiring words make sense. Something deep inside her feels right. It's in her gut again and she knows to always trust her gut.

Be great at what you do. Always try to be better, and never, think you are finished.

These words ring true to Madison's heart.

Wow! What incredible words, she thinks. Madison reads the entire five-page statement. Nina articulates a vision that leaves Madison in awe. Her business concept sounds amazing.

Madison immediately composes a response and is anxious to set up a meeting.

∻   ∻   ∻

Dear Nina,

Thank you for your beautiful statement. Your words are truly inspiring. The things you have written are so close to my thoughts. Beauty and makeup are my passions, but I think these things tie into bigger issues. I would like to think that we are confidence builders and have a responsibility to show women how to present themselves to the world. When a woman looks good, she feels good. There are many definitions of beauty, and I want to explore all of these venues. Just tell me where and when we can meet and I will be there.

Kindest Regards,
Madison K.

∻   ∻   ∻

Madison hits send, and a sense of confidence comes over her. She knows that a woman who could write so eloquently and honestly must be the kind of person who could be a mentor, and the connection she feels to Nina's words settle into her mind. She closes her laptop and reaches for a box filled with new products that she ordered online. She loves the excitement of trying new things.

Chapter 5

MADISON HAS A FABULOUS VINTAGE dresser from the 1930s that she refinished with a harlequin hot-pink and black pattern. This is where she tries all her new makeup products. She has affixed a beautiful lighting system around the elegant mirror and has the perfect setting for makeup day or night. She is happy and calm and begins to open her products. She hears a familiar sound. It is her cell phone singing Rihanna. Kia is calling.

"Hey K." She answers in an upbeat tone. Kia sounds euphoric and starts blabbering about this amazing apartment that she looked at. She was put in charge of finding the girls a place to live in New York City. Madison loves her enthusiasm and is glad that she has called.

"Madison K. my girlfriend you will die when you see this place I scored for us. It is simply heaven on earth. And on top of everything it is a four story walk up, so I am sure we will never gain an ounce."

Kia is a beautiful African American girl. She is not tall like Madison and Jade, and she has real weight issues. Kia has inherited her mother's hefty genes and is constantly fighting the battle of the bulge. Madison always has the quintessential five-pound gain-and-loss issues that all girls can relate to. Madison laughs and thanks Kia for helping to keep her trim. They both agree that Jade will have to eat more often just to keep from disappearing. They also agree that they are secretly very jealous of that prospect. If only they had such a problem. Madison wants to know every detail of the apartment.

"Well, it's not exactly an apartment." Says Kia. She then assures Madison that she will love it, and that she and Jade can decorate it to perfection. She begins to describe a beautiful brownstone located on the Upper West Side.

She articulates to perfection a building that was built in the 1920s with ornamental architecture and original detailing. She speaks of the stone carvings on the front of the building and the hardwood floors. Madison slows her down.

"Kia! Just how much does this place cost? Are you insane? This sounds ridiculous and very expensive."

Kia, who happens to be the daughter of a prominent attorney, is a private school kid, who sometimes forgets that Madison does not come from the means that she does. And while she is certainly not a snob, she has never had to live on a budget. Madison can't get Kia to stop describing and start talking.

"Come on, K, we agreed that we had a budget and we were all going to stick to it. You know that this sounds ridiculous and as of right now I do not even have a paying job, let alone the ability to handle something like this." Kia stops Madison's responsible good-girl speech and intervenes with an interesting fact.

"Listen, Mads, there is this client of my dad's, and he loves my dad. You know everyone loves my dad, and anyway, he kind of owes my dad a favor, and he has tons of property in New York. Sooooo…. he is giving us an amazing deal. You know what they say, it's not what you know, but….."

Madison interrupts. "Kia, you didn't say okay without talking to us, did you? Please tell me you didn't." Madison knows Kia and she knows that Kia is a bit spoiled. She is smart, works hard, and is a good kind person, but she gets everything she wants, even when she doesn't ask for it. Madison tries to explain to Kia that the other half doesn't always get what they want exactly when they want it. Kia, who is always light and jovial, disagrees lovingly with Madison.

"Oh Madison this is just good luck. For once in your life, take something that is good and don't over-think it. I promise you that this is a really great break. Anyway, what's wrong with a little help?"

This kind of situation always makes Madison feel uncomfortable. Since the girls were kids, Kia, has always given over-the-top gifts and extravagant experiences to Madison. Madison appreciates everything that her friend has done for her, but she does not like to live beyond her means. Since the loss of her father, she and her mom have had to keep to a tight budget. She is certainly not suffering, but she is definitely middle class. Jade and Kia both went to private school, had housekeepers, and have had all the extra benefits that go along with being affluent.

Madison does not have a jealous bone in her body, and is truly grateful for all that she has. But at times she has to remind her girls that the real world is a place where most people live. She finally agrees to at least look at the place, but reminds Kia that some things are just, too much. Kia yeses Madison and tells her that she is on her way with the paperwork. She assures Madison that once she sees the place, she will succumb to its perfection.

Madison knows that Kia is one who does not take no for an answer. She has a real dilemma now and has to handle this situation appropriately. She decides to put these thoughts aside for the moment. Madison hangs up the phone and continues rummaging through her box.

She lays out six items and one bottle immediately catches her eye. It's the new Katy Perry fragrance Purr. It is an adorable purple glass bottle in the shape of a Siamese cat. She has an entire collection of modern and vintage perfume bottles. They adorn a beautiful hand painted cabinet in her bathroom. Sometimes she buys the fragrance even if she does not like the scent because she is such a sucker for beautiful bottles.

She sprays and recognizes this scent. She is sure that it is very similar to the original Ed Hardy aroma. She has all the Ed Hardy scents. Fruity is definitely good. She even smells a bit of grape, and likes the assimilation to the color. These kinds of parallels work for her. It's a Madison oddity, or what she refers to as a Madisonism. She will definitely review Purr.

Next she comes across a new bronzer from Too Faced Cosmetics, Peach Leopard. Too Faced is one of her favorite brands. It embodies all of the criteria that Madison loves which are looks, concept, and content. She loves the packaging, but assures her readers that the products are exceptional. As she continues examining her products, Zsa Zsa starts barking. Jade is here.

Madison is surprised, as Jade enters the room.

"Jade! What's going on? Why are you here? Not that I am not glad to see you; I just wasn't expecting you." Madison's keen sense of the untrustworthy smells a set-up. Jade is in an unusually jovial state.

"Well, I am sure by now that you have talked to Kia, and I wanted to be here to see the pictures and details of this insane brownstone."

"Jade," Madison asserts a concerning voice. "We agreed that we were going to get a real place that we could all afford, and not something that was over-the-top. Jade, you have to back me up on this. I have a budget, and I really need to stay within that budget. I understand that you guys can do more, but I want this to be fair and even, and I can't accept an unfair proportion. I really need you to understand this."

"Mads, listen, I spoke with Kia extensively, and she really assures me that her dad was able to get this for an unheard of price. He supposedly does tons of business with the guy who owns it. This guy owes Mr. Donnelly, because he saved him a ton of money on this major case.

He just wanted to help out Mr. Donnelly's daughter. He heard she was going to NYU, and he offered. The price is in our range and really Madison we would be crazy to turn this down. You can't look at everything one way. Look, I am your best friend, and I understand where your head is, but I assure you that this is right, and it is a great opportunity for all of us. We only have this deal for one year and after that, we will probably have to move midtown or downtown. I am telling you, I have seen what's out there. It is not pretty. We would have to be insane not to take this. Just suck it up and say okay."

Madison is stoic. She hates to surrender to the tag team of Jade and Kia, but she does know that they are probably right. She just always feels like they have to lower themselves to her. She hates the whole money thing as it makes her very uncomfortable.

"Okay Jade, let's just say I will look at it. No promises though." She looks right into Jade's eyes and makes her promise to consider her thoughts as well. Jade agrees, and Kia bursts through the door. Kia is a force of uncontrolled energy. She whips out paperwork, cell phone pictures, and actual glossy pictures of this magnificent brownstone.

Kia is sure that when Madison sees this living space she will give in. Madison hits Kia with the fact that she does not even have a paying job or an internship secured. She also reminds Kia that she promised that when she was put in charge of this task that she would not inject any of her usual shenanigans. Kia quips back at her that this is meant to be and they would have to be crazy not to at least consider this. Jade calms the two of them.

"Let's just wait to see it. There is no sense in going crazy, when we have not even been in the actual space or even seen the neighborhood."

Jade, who is not the usual arbitrator, quiets them both with a proposition of going to the city for the day and checking things out. The thought of New York City brings them all to the same happy place. Since the girls were in their mid-teens they made a trip to the city, the first Saturday of every month. They loved to explore Broadway, the museums, the restaurants, and of course the shopping. They loved everything that defined New York City. They were sure at a very young age that this would someday be their home. Madison now exhausted from the banter agrees to do a wait-and-see. Jade and Kia, are confident that they have her. But they quickly change the subject and make their way over to Madison's dresser.

The girls love to explore the dresser that is Madison's think tank. They can always count on some fabulous new product they must have. The girls begin fussing with her newly opened goodies. Kia is the first to distract.

"Oh my god, I love this perfume. Love this bottle! It's the new Katy Perry isn't it?"

Kia douses herself immediately. Jade rolls her eyes and gags, as she does not like this fruity fragrance. One of Jade's major pet peeves is over-perfuming. She truly despises when strong fragrances invade her senses. She definitely keeps her choices light and she is sure that this is a scent she does not like.

"Ugh that is definitely not for me."

Madison assures Jade that Kia has just over-sprayed and that it is a nice summer scent. Jade adamantly disagrees. The girls continue to exchange ideas and play with the products.

"Remember the time when we broke an entire bottle of that Angel perfume on Madison's dresser? Says Kia. Oh my god, poor Madison. Her room stunk for a week."

"I hate that perfume," Jade chimes in.

Madison jokingly reminds them that she could never fairly review this one and that it never did make the list of Madison's favorites. They laugh and continue to talk about many more unforgettable memories.

They also discuss the upcoming trip to the city. Kia is already on the computer checking the train schedules.

"Let's just go tomorrow. I want to get this taken care of as soon as we can. My dad said that all we have to do is agree, and he will do all the paperwork," Kia says. Madison gives her the eyes, and then shoots another look toward Jade. Madison just continues to play with the products ignoring both of her girlfriends.

Madison is a bit angry, so she knows that she better just say nothing. She allows herself time to calm down, and within a few minutes, she is her fun and frantic self. Kia receives a text from her dad and is able to secure a visit to the brownstone tomorrow. The girls agree to go, and as always, they are excited for a trip to their favorite city.

Madison is tired and decides to turn in early. Her friends leave, and she gives Zsa Zsa a quick walk and grabs a bottle of water. She wants to apply a mini facial before she hits the pillow. As she is putting on her products, she gets distracted and thinks of Nina. She decides to check her e-mail, just in case there is a response. When she finds no new e-mails, she calms herself and tries not to panic. She finishes her mini beauty regimen and goes to bed. Tomorrow is a big day. She smiles as she thinks of a day in New York.

Chapter 6

TODAY IS TUESDAY, AND THE girls are en route to the city. It is 6:00 a.m., and Trenton Station is mobbed. Madison keeps Zsa Zsa in a fabulous black bejeweled doggie bag. This bag was definitely a splurge, but it has earned its pay. She takes Zsa in it everywhere, and it looks completely fabulous. Zsa Zsa knows to behave, be quiet, and to chill, when she is in the bag. She knows that as long as she is docile and well behaved, she will have a front-row seat to Madison's life. The girls have an 8:00 a.m. showing with Mr. Matthews, the owner of the brownstone. He has made room in his busy schedule to show the brownstone to the girls personally.

Mr. Matthews has great respect for Mr. Donnelly and is excited to meet Kia. Kia is used to the royal treatment and knows that her dad must be some kind of lawyer, as everyone seems to treat Mr. Donnelly cordially. While she knows that she is fortunate, she has always been appreciative and gracious. These are two of Kia's great attributes, and the girls agree that she will make a great politician one day. Kia has impressive people skills and greatly respects her father's connections. She knows how to handle the most delicate situations, and like her father, it seems everyone loves her. She also knows, that while her father gives her all the luxuries and extra comforts in life, he definitely expects a lot from his eldest daughter, and Kia never wants to disappoint him.

The girls are a bit quiet this morning, maybe a bit tired from the previous day's excitement. They make their way to the train platform, grab a bench, and just quietly stare at the bustling crowd around them. Madison and Jade are true people watchers. They love to redress and makeover the different people in their heads. Madison tends to focus on style and makeup and Jade just redresses everyone. Jade is one tough critic, and it seems no one gets it right. Many times Jade and Madison argue about this issue, where Madison tries to find the positive and Jade, usually holds her ground.

Jade is sure that she can make the world a much more visually appealing place, at least in her mind. She laughs to herself as she sees the outdated and poorly dressed women in the station. She wants to give them instant makeovers. Jade is the judge and jury when it comes to fashion and she always travels with her metaphoric gavel. Her goal is to educate as many women as she can about fit, proportion, and style. The train station is definitely a great place to find strong candidates for her mission. As always, Jade keeps her thoughts to herself, at least for now, unlike Madison, who usually verbalizes her passions. This might be the time that Madison needs her filter. As the train approaches, Madison makes sure to quiet Zsa Zsa.

As the girls enter the train, they can't help but to notice the upgrading of the New Jersey

Transit System. It now has a bi-level and is clean and bright. The last time they went into New York they had really noticed the decline of the trains and even thought about taking Amtrak instead. The girls grab a four-seat unit so that they can face each other, and Madison puts Zsa Zsa on the empty seat by the window. She isn't really sure if her dog is actually allowed on the train so she makes sure she hides her baby with a light raincoat. The girls are still a bit tired, and for now, they are quiet.

The train is packed. So many people take the morning train to get to their New York jobs. Madison is impressed with what she considers a fairly stylish crowd. Still, many women on this train could use her expertise. That she is sure of. The train is still filling up, so the parade of interesting people holds the girls' interest.

A professional-looking middle-aged woman approaches the girls and asks them if she can sit in the seat that looks unoccupied. She sees a bag, but of course does not see Zsa Zsa. Madison has no problem putting Zsa's bag under her seat, and kindly agrees to do so. The woman is immaculately dressed, but definitely has on way too much blush. Her hair is old school, and her makeup is outdated. Madison refers to this as Bubby makeup, and she sees it far too often. It is when women get used to wearing the same makeup for more than ten years, and they do not even realize that they need to update and change with the times.

Madison continues to examine the woman and does everything to conceal her wandering eyes. She is sure that this woman could look so much younger with the proper cosmetics. But for now, she zips her lips. The girls are all smiles, and they start their chatter.

"Oh by the way," says Kia. " I made a lunch reservation at Pastis, a very awesome restaurant in the meat-packing district. I was there recently with my dad, and I am sure you guys will love it. Oh, and I am treating."

Madison starts to open her mouth and then realizes that this is a battle she can't win. Kia continues that she never gave the girls a graduation present and she wants to treat them for lunch. Sometimes, the girls, especially Madison, have no choice but to give in to Kia. They know that all too often it's just not worth it to argue.

Jade is occupied with the New York Times and just agrees.

Madison continues to scan the woman next to her. She tells the woman that she loves her suit, and that the Italian fabric with its tasteful print, is just gorgeous. The woman smiles politely and begins to converse with Madison.

"So, where are you girls headed?" the woman asks. Madison, and now Kia, are engaged. They love socializing, and they just jump in.

"Well" Kia says, "we are on our way to the city to check out a place to live. We all just graduated high school and are starting college in New York."

"Oh how nice" the woman replies. "Where are you going?"

"Well," Kia continues, "Madison, is going to Hunter College and Jade is going to the Fashion Institute of Technology," and then she beams that she will be attending NYU. The woman raises her brow as if to be impressed.

"Wow these are all great achievements. You young ladies should be very proud of your accomplishments."

The girls have now all introduced themselves, and the woman introduces herself as Susan Cummings. She also informs them that she is a-practicing attorney and that she teaches a legal class at NYU.

Kia bursts out "Oh my god, that is my dream! NYU Law School." She continues to babble that that is her dad's alma mater, and it is her ultimate goal to go there. Kia reaches out to shake the woman's hand and continues to chat about her excitement. The woman now turns to Madison.

"So tell me what are you taking at Hunter College?"

Madison replies that she is an artist and a creative girl, and she is currently looking for an internship in the beauty industry. She professes her love for cosmetics, skincare, and the art of beauty. The woman tells Madison that while she has always been book smart, she never quite had a flair for cosmetics. Her statement instantly opens the door for Madison, and she begins to give her beauty advice.

She approaches Susan in a likeable delicate manner and suggests a mini makeover on the train. Susan is a bit hesitant, but Madison works her charm. She takes out her large cosmetics bag and starts to give the woman some lessons. She reaches over to blend her blush, and the woman recoils a bit.

"Oh god, I am so sorry." Madison shrinks back. "I just have this OCD thing and when I see something that I think needs fixing, I just want to fix it."

The woman apologizes and tells her she just wasn't sure what Madison was doing. She then agrees to let Madison fix her makeup. Madison continues with purpose and explains how Susan can get a great natural look and also gain a more youthful appearance.

Jade is still engrossed in her newspaper, and Kia is firing rapid questions at the woman. The girls are in full gear. Madison continues to remake the woman she now knows as Susan, and the time quickly dissolves. She then whips out her very large lighted compact mirror and shows Susan the results. Susan Cummings is delightfully surprised. She looks completely different and she is impressed with the results.

"Wow, you are incredible." Says Susan. "Can I take you home with me?" She laughs. "Okay, you have to show me how you did that. I really look good, maybe a bit younger. You're a sweetheart," she says with affection. "I can't believe how much better I look. Thank you."

Madison gets this reaction every time she does someone's makeup. She has a real talent and loves making women look beautiful. She gets so much satisfaction when she can make a real difference. Susan Cummings is officially remade.

"Madison, do you have a card or something?" asks Susan. Madison realizes that she does not have a card or any information about her magazine. *No worries* she thinks, she will just write down her blog and magazine info, and give it to Susan. She tells Susan that anytime she needs help to just e-mail her. Susan assures her that she could never do this herself, but she will definitely get out and buy the products that Madison has used on her. She assures Madison that she will try, but knows that she does not have Madison's talent. Madison reinforces the fact that Susan can learn these few simple tricks.

"Last stop New York City, Penn Station," the girls hear in a muffled speaker. Susan thanks the girls for an enjoyable and enlightening ride. She hands each of the girls her business card and invites them to reach out to her any time. She looks at Kia and wishes her good luck and also repeats her offer for any help she might need on campus. Everyone on the train is now standing and the girls rise as well. They say their good-byes and exit the train.

Madison straps on her doggie bag and gently nuzzles Zsa Zsa, just to let her know that she is here and Zsa Zsa is safe. She takes out her perfectly matching leash and her hot pink printed poop bags. She leaves the girls at the corner and takes Zsa Zsa to the other side of the train station. She cleans up after her girl and quickly rejoins her friends.

The girls easily hail a taxi. It is a gorgeous day and the streets are full. They jump in, and Madison hands perfectly articulated directions to the cab driver. She knows that if this place is even half as great as Kia professes, she does not have a chance. She gets a guilty feeling every time something goes right for her. She is not sure why this is but she always feels that she has to work harder to earn things. She jokingly blames her mom for this flaw. She laughs to herself and tries to get it out of her head.

Traffic is fairly light, and the girls pull up to this ridiculously beautiful facade. It is 7:54 a.m., and they have arrived at 218 West 79th Street.

This place is gorgeous, Madison thinks to herself as she stares at the beautifully restored building. Madison can't believe that there is a possibility that she could live in this place and can't help but gawk, with her mouth wide open.

Another taxi pulls up, and an older, hefty man, who is a bit disheveled, exits the cab. Mr. Matthews immediately recognizes Kia from all of the pictures he has seen in Mr. Donnelly's office. He approaches the girls with a kind smile and reaches out his hand.

"Hello girls, I am Dominic Matthews. Welcome to my place." He motions to them to follow and swiftly moves up the marble steps to the imposing front door. Once inside Mr. Matthews excitedly begins to converse with them. He immediately reaches out to Kia with a giant bear hug. Madison and Jade smirk and watch, as, Kia is consumed by the very large man.

"I feel like I know you Kia. I have spent many hours in your father's company, and he is always speaking about his beautiful angel, Kia. This is one of my favorite properties," he says proudly. "When I heard that Mr. Donnelly's daughter was coming to New York City, I just had to extend my gratitude. You know, Kia, your father saved me from losing a lot of my properties. He is an incredible lawyer and a heck of a human being."

Kia is used to this kind of behavior, but Madison and Jade are a bit overwhelmed. The girls now focus on the grand interior of this home.

Madison glances at the marble staircase and the cast- iron railings. She stands frozen look-ing at all of the original details in the ceiling's moldings. She is sure that this place has been completely restored, and while it looks old, it has been completed to perfection. Even with her moral fiber, who could say no to this?

The guilt hits Madison hard. She feels irresponsible for even being here, and her emotions get the best of her. She actually begins to well up. Jade notices the water in Madison's eyes, and she nudges Madison and gives her the, "it's going to be great" face. Madison is completely overcome by the grandeur of this experience. She excuses herself and goes outside to walk Zsa Zsa.

Kia is still chatting with Mr. Matthews and does not take notice of Madison's expression. Mr. Matthews encourages the girls to look around and get a feel for the place. He also assures them that this is a lucky situation. Because of his legal problems, he is unable to sell this property until next year. So the fact that he can do this for his friend Mr. Donnelly is a great feeling for him. He continues talking and then excuses himself. He gives Kia a key and tells her to just lock the door when they have finished their tour. He apologizes that he must leave for another appointment. He assures Kia that they can move in as soon as they are ready and that he would be thrilled to have the girls as tenants. As soon as Mr. Matthews leaves, Kia, bursts out with a scream.

"Oh my god, do you believe this place?" She starts running around the house completely freaking out. Jade needs to school Kia a bit and gives her a piece of her mind.

"Kia, you did not say that we were going to be living in a fricken' palace. Jesus, Kia, did you see the look on Madison's face? She is embarrassed. Frankly, I am a bit suspect of this whole thing. What the hell did your dad do for this guy? I mean, this is like a $10 million brownstone. How the heck are we supposed to explain living here?"

Kia responds. "Look Jade I am telling you that we are still paying for this place. My dad said that all you guys have to come up with is $1000 per month and that he will take care of the rest. Mr. Matthews worked out a trade for my dad's services. I mean I have been up here looking for a while.

"So basically your dad is paying for this?" Jade says angrily. "If Madison knew what you were up to she would have a fit. Look, I want to get a place just as much as you do, but I think this is a bad idea."

"Jade, I have to tell you that my dad assures me that Mr. Matthews already owes him, and that this is the only way he can get paid at all because, of Mr. Matthews financial situation or something like that. Whatever it is we would have to be insane to say no to this. I say yes, absolutely yes."

Jade reminds Kia that she promised Madison that she would be a bit realistic when they discussed the prospect of living in New York. Kia reminds Jade that sometimes, good luck is just good luck and today is their lucky day. Madison re-enters the brownstone.

"Well I guess I can't argue that the neighborhood isn't definitely safe." Madison smiles, as she gathers her thoughts and decides to look upon the fortune of being Kia's friend. The girls huddle together, and they all hug. Kia puts her arm around Madison.

"Listen, Mads, let's just say we had some good luck with some good friends today. Remember, we only have this place for one year, and then it is going on the market. So what if we live a bit high for our first year. Hey, it's only a house, and we still have to work hard to meet all of our bills, and of course we have to semi-furnish this place."

Madison is quick to remind Kia that this is the end of her reign, and that from now on, they will all make decisions as a team and that they must respect each other's opinions. Madison reluctantly agrees to live in the beautiful brownstone. The girls continue to explore and make other decisions about who will be where and what tasks they will each be in charge of. Madison notices a quaint room off the kitchen. She completely loves the space as it is small but has very high ceilings. Madison is a tall girl and loves rooms that are tall, like her. She just likes the feel of a soaring ceiling in conjunction with her being. She has found her room, and it is a dream. The girls continue to explore the beautiful property and all four magnificent floors. They each call their parents and describe the beauty that is before them. They have succumbed to excitement.

Chapter 7

AS MADISON TAKES OUT HER Blackberry, she notices a new e-mail. It is from Nina.

✄ ✄ ✄

Hi Madison,

I am in town all this week and would love to meet with you. Let me know what works best for you.

Regards,
Nina Hagen

✄ ✄ ✄

Madison thinks to herself that maybe as Kia has stated, today really is her lucky day. A quick response is in order.

❧ ❧ ❧

Hi Nina,

As crazy as it may seem I am actually in New York today. Would you have any time to meet? I am free all afternoon.

Kind Regards,
Madison K.

❧ ❧ ❧

Madison quickly shares the news with her girls, and they are all in agreement that this day must be meant to happen and that Madison is definitely going to work for Nina Hagen. Madison begins to believe them but still as always, she has some doubts.

The girls make their calls. Kia calls her dad and immediately thanks him for this opportunity and tells him that she knows how lucky she is. Kia loves her dad, and expresses that often. He is truly her idol. Madison also reaches her mom and tells her of the amazing brownstone. She warns her that it is a crazy situation and prepares her for the shock when she comes up on moving day.

Madison now gets in her OCD mode. She begins to make her lists. She informs Kia and Jade what they have to do.

"Okay, girls, if we are going to do this we need to get a few things straight. Kia, you will be in charge of hooking up the phones and Internet. Jade, you will contact the electric company. You need to get us some established credit. Let's try to do the rest of this on our own. Thanks to Mr. Donnelly, we have an amazing place to live, but we have much to do," Madison now feels her Blackberry vibrate and pulls it from her pocket. It is Nina.

⚜ ⚜ ⚜

Hi Madison,

What great luck! Can we meet around 2:00 p.m.? I am in the process of opening my new *store and I would love to meet with you there. It is located at 60th and Lexington, right next to Bloomingdales. My office is the little door to the left of the store. It is not yet opened, so ring the bell.*

Nina

જ⁄ર જ⁄ર જ⁄ર

Madison confirms, and she now has a date with destiny. She gathers her girls to tell them the news. Kia grabs Madison and tells her that this is it and that she is going to make it from here. She is completely confident that this was all meant to be and that Madison and Nina are going to make history. Kia does not know how right she is.

It is now 10:45 a.m., and the girls have thoroughly examined every nook and cranny of 218 West 79th. Madison suggests window-shopping in the meatpacking district. She has been reading about the new stores in the area. The girls like the idea, since that is where they are having lunch. They want to make sure that they manage their time well and do not make Madison one second late for her meeting with Nina. They exit the brownstone and check and recheck that they have locked the door.

Madison takes Zsa Zsa out of her bag and hooks up her leash. The girls begin their long walk from 79th Street. It is a gorgeous day, and the longer they walk the better chance they have of not spending money that they don't have. They walk down to the West Side and along the river. The streets of New York are packed; *it is funny how a beautiful day makes New York look more populated than Tokyo,* Jade thinks. Tokyo is where her mom is from and Jade frequently visits her grandparents there.

The girls have now walked fifty blocks, and they are really feeling it in their shoe choices. Madison is prepared of course as she always carries her Footzyrolls. These are tiny roll up flats that you keep in your bag when your feet start to hurt. Madison's handbag is like a MacGyver fashion emergency kit. There is always some great gadget or beauty product that just makes life easier. They are just entering Chelsea and are happy to check out the stores. Jade is immediately attracted to the Alexander McQueen store and insists that this be their first stop. He is one of Jade's favorite designers, and when the girls enter the store, they make the immediate connection. They continue to browse, and Jade even tries on a jacket. She explains to the girls that while his clothing is super pricy, the design, fabric, and construction warrant the hefty prices.

Kia and Madison agree, and then they also agree that they are completely out of their league. Jade tells the girls that these are clothes that are worth having and that if they just buy one or two items a year they will last forever. The girls appreciate Jade's passion but can't imagine spending that amount of money on a garment. It is now close to 12:00 noon, and the girls are starving. Pastis is just a few blocks away. The threesome make their way toward the crowded restaurant and can't wait to sit. They have expelled a lot of energy this morning and are completely famished. They walk to the reception area and check in. The noise level is definitely high, but the energy is exciting and fun.

Madison is very careful to hide Zsa Zsa, when they are seated. She knows that dogs are not allowed in restaurants, but she has no choice. She makes sure that her dog will not be seen. Besides, Zsa Zsa knows the drill. Stay quiet in the bag, and a tasty treat awaits at the end.

Madison loves eating out, and she always appreciates a beautiful presentation. She notices every detail. She loves the creative way food is displayed on a plate. Kia is the first to decide on her meal. The girls like her choice and they all order burgers and fancy French fries.

They find it funny that none of them became vegetarians, something they once talked about as kids. They sometimes have a guilty conscience, but they do like their meat. Madison hates the fact that she has to even think about what she eats. She and Kia are always trying out some weird new diet, but today, she tells herself to just enjoy the dang French fries. Today is a memorable experience and these three best friends have much to say.

Nina is now in her office. It is 1:30 p.m., and she prepares for her meeting with Madison. Her new store is under construction, her website is now up and running, and she has just secured a fabulous new store manager. Julia Parker is a junior at Queens College and is working her way through school. She is a fun young woman who loves makeup and definitely has the gift of gab. She is organized and frankly, just a nice girl. Nina is pleased with her prospects thus far.

Nina has prepared a list of questions for Madison and is excited at the idea of hiring her. She is also in negotiations with the brands that she wants to carry in her store and some of these companies are tough to deal with. Nina has always been on the corporate end of business, and now that she is becoming a retailer, she is seeing the challenges and the difficulties that lie in front of her. Nina has taken on quite a challenge, and she wants BLC to be the best in the business. She figures that it will take at least thirty employees to run her 5,000-square-foot, concept store, and they will all have to be very well trained. Nina is a very detailed and aggressive woman and is sure to get the staff that she wants.

It is now 1:40 p.m., and the girls have finished their lunch. Kia and Jade remain talking and Madison exits and jumps into a waiting taxi. She leaves Zsa Zsa with the girls and makes them promise to take care of her baby. They laugh and remind her that they are Zsa Zsa's aunties and would never let anything happen to her.

"Sixtieth and Lexington," she nicely tells the cab driver. Oddly, Madison finds herself calm. Probably her interview with Leonard was the worst day of her life, but today could be the best. She decides to be positive, and she knows that regardless of the outcome of today's meeting with Nina, she has to step up her magazine and try to grow her readership. She is starting to see her path and wants so much to achieve success. She remembers something that her father told her before he died. *Never, ever, ever, give up. If you believe, they will believe.* It was a strange dichotomy for young Madison, and she chose to believe instead of being angry. It was a hard day for the then eleven-year-old, but she always knew that his words would mean something in her life. Madison is lost in thought, and the cab driver reminds her that she has arrived.

"Oh, sorry." Madison says. She pays her tab and gets out. She is directly in front of Bloomingdales and sees that the store next to it has its windows covered with paper. She remembers the fabulous logo that is stamped on the paper. Now she is very excited. She sees a door with a bell. It is 2:05 p.m., but she knows that by New York standards, she is right on time. She rings the buzzer, and it buzzes back. She opens the door.

There is a walk-up in front of her, and she starts to climb. She gets to the first level, and she sees the door that says "office." *It certainly does not look imposing.* She opens the door and sticks her head inside.

"Hello?" she calls out. Nina waves her in, as she is on the phone. The office is very messy, and there are boxes everywhere. Nina finishes her phone call and greets Madison.

"Madison, I am so excited to meet with you." Nina extends her hand. She seems much less intimidating than on the day they first met. She is softer and definitely warmer. Madison does consider that the day they met, she did knock her to the floor, and decides that she likes this version of Nina better. Nina leads Madison back to her work area. She apologizes for the mess and tells her that it has been a hectic few weeks. She just recently occupied this space and has everything to do.

"Ah, Madison K. I must tell you that I have been doing my homework, and I think you have a special talent and a genuine persona that is sorely lacking in the beauty industry. Tell me more about yourself."

Madison begins to speak, and as always, goes into her manic mode.

"I love makeup and I love the idea of real genuine information about how a product works. I think that it is important to know why one product is really better than another. I am talking about the real truth. I want to explore all the possibilities, but I also want to acknowledge that the experience is everything. I mean shopping with your mom, or your sisters, or your friends, is real quality time, and memories are often being made. I just think that the world has forgotten about the human being. I really want to bring authenticity and humanity into the beauty industry. I mean in the end it has to be about the fun. Doesn't it?"

She looks for a sign from Nina, but she isn't sure of the reaction on Nina's face.

"I can't explain it. I just have such a passion for it." Madison shrinks a bit and questions Nina. "Am I making sense?"

Nina is actually just staring at Madison as if she has seen a ghost. Madison quiets down, as she is sure that she has lost Nina. Nina snaps back and reaches out with a hug. She is so impressed by the passion that Madison has just demonstrated and is, frankly, speechless. She now composes herself and what she says shocks Madison. She begins by saying that she has a lot of business and life experience and she does not often meet a vibrant and unique individual like her, especially at her young age. She tells Madison that she was once as passionate as she, and twenty years in corporate almost destroyed her. She is completely in awe of the honesty and integrity in Madison's words and what she knows instantly to be Madison's heart.

"Madison, today is your lucky day and mine as well. With all that you have accomplished in your young years and with my connections and savvy, I truly believe we could make a great team."

Madison starts her waterworks again. Nina actually fills up a bit as well. Nina and Madison talk of business, life, family and fun. After about an hour Nina knows that she must have Madison on her team and that she must be honest and fair to Madison's naiveté. Madison remembers Nina's statement and just knows that whatever Nina's got planned, it must be huge.

Nina gives Madison a contract that she had drawn up, just in case Madison turned out to be the girl that she thought she was. Nina now gets a bit serious.

"Madison it is so clear to me that you are a perfect match for my company, and I believe that we can do great things together. I have written an agreement, that I think is fair and will still give you complete ownership of your magazine. It is a true business agreement and there is a lot to digest. Please take it home and read it. I have thought a lot about you, and I want you to be a part of BLC. You're fresh and innovative, and most of all you're honest. I have been around enough dishonest people to know a jewel when I see one. I think you are special."

Madison is now shaking, and she is excited and scared all at once. She has so many questions that are now racing through her mind. She is sure that she wants this but has learned from past experience that she must read thoroughly all that has been presented to her. Nina is sure that Madison is the girl she wants and knows that she must allow Madison the time she needs to understand what is in the contract. Madison thanks Nina and reaches out to her with a hug. She promises her that she wants to work for BLC, but that she must read the contract thoroughly and then she will give her an immediate response. Nina is happy to see that Madison has learned from her experience and tells her to take the time she needs and to be sure that she is in agreement with the offer.

Kia and Jade continue to shop in the Chelsea area as they anxiously await a call from Madison. Jade's phone is the first to vibrate.

OMG ALL GOOD! Kia's phone has a duplicate message. And now another message arrives.

Where r u guys? I am on my way☺

Kia and Jade are happy and relieved. They live and breathe for each other's accomplishments, and they know that Madison deserves this opportunity. They have watched her evolve and never miss a step, even when faced with adversity. They have always had an "all for one, and one for all" mentality, and when one succeeds, it seems they all do.

Madison stands outside Nina's store beaming. She knows in her heart that this is the right place for her, but her mind is still racing. She flags down a taxi and heads for Chelsea. She looks down at the contract and realizes that it is quite detailed. She knows now from her last experience not to over-analyze these words. She will leave that to a professional. Mr. Donnelly will surely help her with this. Ugh, another guilty moment for Madison, as she thinks of asking for another favor from Mr. Donnelly. She will first take this contract home and go over it with her mom. Maybe she won't have to bother Mr. Donnelly. She is too excited to focus right now. She looks out of the window and takes in the sights of New York City. She is having a completely happy moment, and she is not going to let her brain ruin it.

Madison's taxi pulls up right in front of the Chelsea Market. The girls are exactly where they said that they would be. That is good news for Mads because the girls often get lost in the fabulous shopping that is New York. She pays the driver and even adds a big tip. She is sure that today is her most lucky day and a strong feeling of self-confidence comes over her. The driver is visibly pleased and verbalizes a very appreciative thank you.

As Madison exits the taxi, she can hardly contain herself. She lifts up Zsa Zsa and then circles her girls with the news. She suggests that they sit for a cup of coffee and digest all that has taken place. She tells them about a fabulous coffee house that caught her eye a few blocks back. She also quickly and firmly tells Kia that it is she who is treating, and that is that. Kia looks impressed and knows that she must agree. Madison takes Zsa for a quick walk and tells the girls to reserve a table in the back.

Madison enters the most adorable vintage café with the most gorgeous cupcakes and treats that she has ever seen. As she walks toward the back she sees a red velvet cupcake with the most beautiful iced pink flower on it. This lovely treat is definitely calling her name. Having already celebrated with French fries, she hesitates just a bit. But that small red velvet cupcake, with its beautifully ornamented flower, just will not let her off the hook.

Madison slides Zsa Zsa's bag under the table and prepares to tell the girls the great news. Jade and Kia start to prod Madison.

"So what's the deal? What did Nina say?" Kia blurts out.

Jade says "Does she want you to keep writing your magazine? What is her concept, anyway? Did you see her store?"

Madison is a bit overwhelmed, and the waitress appears just in time for her to gather her thoughts. An edgy emo-looking girl approaches. Madison can't help but to stare at her many tattoos, piercings, and ear gages. They really freak her out. *She is a pretty girl,* Madison thinks, and for the life of her, can't understand the ear gage thing. She never quite understood the body art thing either; but that might have a lot to do with the fact that she is terrified of needles. Madison tries to control her wandering eyes and focuses on her order. She succumbs to the red velvet cupcake, and the girls order from the menu. The waitress leaves, and Madison begins to tell her tale.

"So it was not what I would call a formal interview. I mean not that I actually know what a formal interview is, but with every fiber of my being, I know that this is meant to be, and this is where I belong. It is like Nina and I are the same person, and we share the same ideals. I am not really even sure what exactly she wants me to do in terms of the actual job, but she has no interest in taking over my magazine, and she is sure that we can build her concept and my magazine at the same time. She was very complimentary of my accomplishments and really appreciative of all that I have done. I can't explain it, but I know that my gut is right on this. The same way I knew when I met with Leonard Grayson. My gut told me that it was definitely wrong, and right now my gut tells me that this is right. I mean I know that I have to get more information and Nina and I are meeting again next week. Oh, and I forgot she had a contract waiting for me."

"Uh let me see that," says Kia. She signals to Madison to hand it over. Then she scolds her a bit. "You did not sign anything, did you?"

Madison laughs. "Come on, Kia I may not be an NYU pre-law student, but I am not stupid. Of course I did not sign anything, and Nina did not ask me to. She was very kind, and she told me to take as much time as I needed to read and understand what she is asking from me and she also encouraged me to take it to a lawyer."

"That would be Daddy." Kia quips.

Madison stops her and tells her that she first wants to read it with her mom, as she does not want to take advantage of Mr. Donnelly. She further reiterates that he has been so amazing to her that she could not ask for one more favor. But Kia goes right at her and reminds her that her father promised Madison's dad that he would always look out for her. Kia also reminds Madison that Mr. Kensington was a good friend of her family's and that if she did not show the contract to her dad, he may not be too happy with her. Kia, always well organized with her words, somehow always leaves Madison without a fight. Madison just agrees and continues telling the details of the meeting. She tells the girls that she never saw the store and that she is planning to meet with Nina next week, when she will find out more about all of the venues of her business.

The girls enjoy their desserts and then decide that it is time to head home. Madison is excited to really read all that is in front of her, and she also decides to put in writing many of the questions that she has for Nina. Today was definitely a good day.

Chapter 8

THE TRAIN RIDE HOME IS much less interesting than the one up into the city. Jade is fully engrossed in her new sketchpad, her only purchase of the day. She keeps busy drawing fabulous looks for the upcoming fall season. She is constantly drawing, and her friends are in awe of her endless ideas. Kia spends most of the ride checking her e-mails and playing on her iPhone. Madison actually nods out for more than half the ride. She wakes about three stops from Trenton. She put her fingers through her hair and is sure she needs a shower. The one thing that Madison really hates about New York is the fact that after a long day in the city, there is what seems to be a dirty residue on her entire body.

She reaches into her magic bag and pulls out her Nupore cucumber wipes. She hands them to Kia and Jade and advises them to wipe off their faces and take off their face makeup. She tells them not to remove their eye makeup as that would be inappropriate and way too messy, but that their faces definitely need to breathe. She is sure that they have a ton of dirt and grit accumulated in their pores. The girls laugh, but agree and do a quick swipe. Madison however thoroughly cleanses her face and neck and even wipes down her arms. She then takes out her Tata Harper floral spray for a fresh dose of botanicals.

The girls realize that they are providing great amusement for the surrounding passengers. Madison notices a few women watching with interest. She quickly acknowledges the women and tells them that these little babies are a must for any handbag. She says that not only do they quickly cleanse the face, and are great for on the go, but they are also all natural. "No irritants, just soft, clean, and fabulous," she says excitedly.

The women listen and even write down the name of the wipes. They ask her about the spray that she just used, and Madison quickly writes it down, along with her name and blog info. They arrive at Trenton Station, and Madison graciously invites them to e-mail her directly. Before leaving, she tells them to close their eyes and their mouths. She then gives them each a spray of the floral hydrating essence.

She assures them that they will be hooked.

"E-mail me and I will give you the facts," she says.

At this point, Jade is dragging Madison away. Jade is tired and has had enough. The girls exit the train smack in the middle of rush hour. It is completely insane in Trenton Station. They walk through the station with purpose, and Jade pulls out the parking ticket for the underground lot. The sun is still shining, and the air is warm. They make their way to Jade's car, chip in for parking, and head home. Kia looks down at her phone and sees a text from Gregg Parker. He asks her if she wants to grab a bite tonight and hang out. Kia smiles as she read this text. Gregg Parker is a very talented and very good-looking baseball player from her school, and is going to Penn State in the fall. Kia has always liked Gregg, and while they have always been friends, she now knows that he is a bit more interested in something beyond that. She is happy and annoyed at the same time.

What took him so long, she thinks? She really doesn't want to start anything right now. She is focused on New York, and he will be five hours away at Penn State. Kia is what one would describe as a serial dater. This girl always has a date, but she has never had a real boyfriend. It seems Kia is quite high-maintenance. *At any rate*, Kia thinks to herself, that it sounds like a fun night.

She informs the girls that she will see Gregg tonight, and they dig at her a bit.

"Okay you man-eater," says Jade, "try to go easy on this guy. He has no idea what he is in for."

Madison quickly scolds Jade and supports the idea of a date with Gregg. Madison has known Gregg for years and really likes him for Kia.

"Hey, Gregg is a good guy and a real gentleman, and he's smart, nice, and has a fabulous body," says Madison. They all agree and laugh.

Jade drops Madison off, and Madison walks Zsa Zsa before she goes inside. Her mom is home today, and Madison is sure she must have an amazing dinner waiting. Tuesday is the day that Madison's mom cooks and she is a fabulous cook. Every Tuesday they have a proper dinner together, and Madison's stomach is excited.

Madison bursts into the house and calls for her mom. She smells the garlic and knows that that must be her favorite: angel hair pomodoro and homemade garlic bread. According to Madison, her mom's garlic bread has no rivals. It is simply the best. She calls out to her mom and tells her that she is just going upstairs to get washed, and she will be down A.S.A.P. Zsa Zsa heads right to the kitchen because this dinner is also Zsa Zsa's favorite. She just loves spaghetti. Madison is cleaned up and ready for the great meal that is ahead of her. She sneaks up behind her mom and gives her a loving hug.

"Yum that smells delicious. I'm so glad today is Tuesday, and you're home. We have lots to talk about."

Madison goes to set the table, but when she walks into the dining room, she sees that her mom has already set all her favorite vintage dishes. She has layered beautiful linens and the plates are eclectically placed to perfection. Madison is in awe of her mom's creativity and loves that she inherited her abilities. *She is so thoughtful and detailed,* Madison thinks. She professes her love for the look, and then they both sit. Her mom has also prepared small Caesar salads, something they both love. Madison is sure that she must have gained a few pounds today, but she puts that thought aside and starts to eat. She takes a few bites and begins with the story of the day.

She is very descriptive about the brownstone and excitedly describes the beautiful facade, as well as the room that will be hers. She then talks about her interview, Nina, and the contract. Her mom listens intently and gives her some very good and very sound advice. They agree to look at the contract tomorrow and continue to eat and talk of the future. Madison's mom assures her that things work out the way they are supposed to. She adds that things may not always be exactly how you want them, but they do work out. She reminds Madison that she has a long road ahead of herself and to try not to overanalyze everything.

Madison's mom knows how passionate and emotional Madison can be and just wants her only daughter to understand that the world is a tough place. She also admits that she has sheltered her daughter from a lot of it.

"Leonard Grayson called here today. He left a message and asked for you to call him back." She says matter-of-factly.

Madison is shocked and wonders why he called her house phone and not her cell. She runs up to check her phone to see if she had any missed calls or voicemails. It seems she does. She decides to put her phone aside for now and to return to her mom, as time with her mom is precious.

Madison makes sure that she makes Zsa Zsa a small bowl of spaghetti. She carefully cuts it up into tiny pieces, and Zsa patiently waits. Her baby has been exceptional today, and she deserves a rewarding dinner. It is now 7:45, and Madison starts to clear the table. Her mom shoos her away and tells her that she is always helping and to just go upstairs and take it easy.

She acknowledges that Madison has had a very full day and would like to see her daughter relax. This is something Madison does not do well, but she reluctantly agrees.

Leonard Grayson is working late again. Faction Cosmetics has started two new divisions, and he has much to do. He is no stranger to hard work, and he did not get where he is today for no good reason. He grew up in Brooklyn and came from a lower-middle-class family. Len, as he likes to be called, has always had his eye on the money prize. He vowed to rule the world one day, and he has clawed and manipulated his way to where he is today. He has been known to be smart, tough, and very manipulative. He is also known to have a great eye for talent and to be the best in the business.

Grayson's secretary has left him with a bundle of new interns coming in. His current concern is PR, as his company has had some negative publicity lately. He sits back and reads the bios and resumes of the hired interns. He is looking for something special. What he finds are many intelligent young people but no stars. He likes the idea of the interns because he can mold them to the Faction way. He also thinks about the young girl from Bucks County. *The one that got away*, as he refers to her. He put in one last call to Madison Kensington, because he is sure that she is just the girl he is looking for.

Social media is exploding, and he knows that he needs this tool for his company. Leonard is smart enough to know that the corporate zombies have very little integrity. He wants to bring a face to Faction, and he wants someone with genuine passion to do it. But he also wants control and Leonard Grayson is used to getting what he wants.

It is now 8:30 p.m., and Madison considers Mr. Grayson's phone call. She figures he is not in the office. Since he left two numbers, she decides to call him at the office number to be polite and respectful, and she is sure that she will be able to leave a message. She is tired and does not want to have a whole conversation tonight. There is an automated system that she has to navigate at his office number. When she finally reaches his extension, she takes a deep breath and prepares to deliver a polite message. She is sure that she does not care for this man, but she does have the good sense to understand that he is a big deal in the industry, and she doesn't want to be rude or burn any bridges. His voicemail does not pick up.

"Leonard Grayson," says a smooth, deep voice with no hint of a Brooklyn accent.

"Oh, uh, Mr. Grayson?" Madison is befuddled.

"Yes, this is he. Can I help you?"

"Oh, hello, Mr. Grayson. I guess I was caught off guard a bit. I didn't, I mean, I just, you know it's late. I'm sorry, this is Madison Kensington."

Grayson smiles and turns on the charm. "Madison, it is funny that you called at this moment. I was just going through my intern list, and I did not see your name on it."

Madison is now more confused.

Grayson continues, "I think maybe I under-estimated you, and I am sorry about the whole contract thing. I guess I just assumed that you understood how Faction worked and that this is just standard procedure. I am a no- nonsense guy and I was sure that you were right for the company."

Now smiling like a Cheshire cat, Grayson delivers the final punch. "Madison I think you have great potential, but without the backing of a large corporation like ours, your magazine and ideas may just get lost in the noise."

Madison now feels nauseous. There is a lump in her throat and a knot in her stomach.

"You have great potential, maybe the best that I have seen in a young woman, but you need the right connections. Faction, my dear Madison, is the right connection."

Madison is silent, Grayson questions if she is still on the line. She is unsure how to respond and decides to just be honest.

"Mr. Grayson after our interview, I felt uncomfortable with the document you gave me. Now, I have to admit that I really did not even fully read this document, but it just did not look right to me."

Mr. Grayson briefly interrupts Madison to also apologize for leaving the Brigade Room, but explains that he really did have another meeting.

Madison continues, "Maybe I reacted wrong, but I have worked so hard on my magazine, and I guess I am just inexperienced and don't really understand what you are offering me. I thought that I was walking into something completely different. I mean, I guess that is my fault; my expectations may be off the mark." She also confesses that she has been offered another job, and that she has not made any decision yet.

Grayson reassures Madison that this is a good thing because Faction is where she belongs. He continues to court her with the things he can do for her career.

She is now feeling sicker. *I guess I am really naïve*, she thinks to herself. She has learned many lessons in the last two weeks, and one of them is that things are just not black and white. But, to her things are either right or they are wrong.

She finishes her conversation with Mr. Grayson and assures him that she will consider his offer. He gives her one week. She runs to the bathroom and throws up her entire meal. She is flush and hot. Her mom hears her and knocks on the bathroom door.

"Are you okay honey?" she asks. Madison emerges from the bathroom paste white. She is definitely not okay. She collapses into her mom's arms and begins to sob.

"I am such a naive lightweight. I guess I really am from la la land. I just know in my gut when things are not right, but how do I make a good decision? She continues to tell her mom of the conversation that she had with Mr. Grayson, and all that Nina had told her. She is so worried that she will make the wrong decision and that at eighteen she could be ruined. Now everyone who loves Madison, and definitely her mom, knows how dramatic Madison can execute a sentence, but she can see that Madison is genuinely upset.

Her mom guides her to her bed and grabs a cool washcloth for her forehead. She lovingly reminds Madison that the dinner she had slaved over all afternoon was now down the drain. They both laugh.

Madison quietly chimes in, "Well, that's one way not to feel guilty about a bad-eating day."

Her mother looks at her sternly and does not find that statement funny at all. She touches her finger to her daughter's nose and reminds her that things always seem better after a good night's sleep. Madison agrees, and while it is only 9:30 p.m., she turns out her light and goes to sleep.

Chapter 9

TODAY IS WEDNESDAY. LAST NIGHT was a rough one. Madison tossed and turned and even had a few nightmares. She knows that she has everything to do and considers pulling the covers over her head and going back to sleep. She realizes that this is definitely not an option and gets out of bed. Zsa Zsa is a bit groggy, and Madison has to nudge her up for her walk. She gently lifts up her girl and heads for the steps. The house is quiet as usual, and today this is good. She has to catch up on her blog and has a ton of e-mails to answer. She takes Zsa out for a quick walk and stops in the kitchen for a bowl of cereal.

She decides to put off all the business of last night and work on her blog. Madison has been dying to write about her new favorite nail polish. She sits at her computer and considers her fans as she composes her thoughts.

First, she writes about the beautiful brownstone and the possibility to be able to share it with her BFFs, and of her recent trip to New York. She tells her fans that she will be starting college in the fall, but that she will continue to bring them what she feels are the best and the brightest of the beauty world. She writes how she was so tired the night before her big New York trip, but the thought of going to the Big Apple with colorless unkempt nails was just not an option.

What a perfect time to try the new polish from Butter London. She mentions that it is three-free, which means that it is free of the three most deadly carcinogens found in nail polish. The culprits are formaldehyde, toluene, and DBP. She describes in perfect detail the special way that Butter glides on with ease and how it definitely does not reek of the awful smell usually associated with nail polish. She even polished Zsa Zsa's nails with it, she tells them excitedly.

She writes of the fabulous topcoat and how it lasted beautifully all through her crazy day in the city. "Not one chip" she enthusiastically tells them. She now looks down at her nails, and they still look perfect. Madison is pleased. She continues to write and share her dining experiences and shopping fun. She ends her thoughts with the fact that she is looking for a New York-based job and encourages her readers to stay tuned. She sends them love as always and signs off.

Madison glances at the piece of paper that is lying on her dresser. She knows that she must address this immediately. She got her writing in and is now completely focused on the contract. She starts to read and so far so good. Madison sees nothing about ownership of her magazine. It is a formal job offer, and it seems that basically Nina wants her to continue doing what she is doing and to do it under the umbrella of the BLC Beauty Corporation.

Madison is shocked at the salary. $40,000 per year for two years guaranteed with the option of negotiation after one year. There is a ton of legal stuff in here, and that scares Madison a bit. She decides that she should probably take Kia up on her offer, or more like her demand, and call Mr. Donnelly, but first she definitely needs a shower. Madison can never start her day without a fragrant bath or shower. She needs it like the air she breathes.

Mr. Donnelly has two magnificent offices. His main office is in the city, and then he has another office in Doylestown, Pennsylvania. He is a licensed attorney in Pennsylvania, New Jersey, and New York. Mr. Donnelly is a big deal in the legal world. That is something that Madison has known since she was a child.

Doylestown is a lovely area located in the heart of Bucks County. The historic town has an elegant atmosphere and all the big cases of Bucks County are tried right at the Doylestown courthouse. Mr. Donnelly is like the mayor here. Everyone knows Matthew Donnelly.

Born and raised in Newtown, PA, Matthew Donnelly is the local boy who made good. He can do no wrong in Bucks County. Wednesdays in Mr. Donnelly's office are completely crazy.

Lawyers enter and leave frequently and interns and paralegals run from task to task. Court is in session, and business is good. Kia is here to see her dad. Mrs. Clarkson, the receptionist, greets her with a smile.

"Kia, I swear you get prettier every time I see you," she says. Mrs. Clarkson has worked for Mr. Donnelly for over fifteen years and is practically part of the family. She has watched Kia and her sisters grow up. She just adores them. "Congratulations!" she says. "I hear you are moving to New York City."

Kia responds with a kind smile and a warm hug. She then signals to Mrs. Clarkson that she can see how busy everyone is and that she is just going to peek in on her dad. Mrs. Clarkson gives her the all-clear sign, and Kia proceeds. She slips into his office and sneaks up behind her dad. She wraps her arms around his back and belly, which has gotten noticeably bigger over the years. She gives him a very loving and proper hug.

"Hi Daddy," Kia is always excited to visit her dad in his office. He seems so important, and she has happy memories of her mom bringing her and her sisters to visit. Her dad was always working when she was young, and things still have not changed. However, when Kia is in the room, Mr. Donnelly is completely focused on his girl. He puts his papers down and takes his glasses off. His baby is here to see him. He completely dotes on Kia, and always has.

"Hey baby, what brings you in so early? I thought you would be out shopping for your new home." He laughs. "Or shopping for well, whatever it is that you girls shop for." Now they both laugh.

Mr. Donnelly is a victim of an all-girl household, and shopping is a major topic in the Donnelly house. Kia gets serious.

"Listen, Dad, I am really concerned about Madison. She got this job offer in the city, but there is this contract, and she is so naive and trusting, and well I just worry, you know? I guess you taught me well, and I just don't want my BFF getting abused. Anyway, you know Madison, and how she always feels so guilty about everything. I just don't want her to feel guilty about asking for a favor. She is already so mad about the brownstone, and you know she always feels like I am trying to take care of her, which of course I am, but she can't really know how much I worry about her, and the fact that she does not have a dad and oh my god, am I making sense?" rambles Kia.

Mr. Donnelly knows exactly what his daughter wants.

"Why don't I call Madison right now?" he says. Kia just smiles and throws her whole body at her dad. "You're the best daddy in the whole world."

"You always understand me. I truly am the luckiest girl in the world," Kia boasts.

Kia picks up the phone and calls Madison. She reminds her dad that she is not here and that she never was. Mr. Donnelly has survived for many years in a house full of women, and he is a very smart man. He winks at Kia, and the pact is made.

Madison steps out of her shower and quickly grabs her favorite pink-and-white Betsey Johnson terrycloth robe. *Nothing like a fabulous shower* she thinks to herself. She wraps her hair in a towel and heads for the bedroom. She sits at her dresser and checks out the face in front of her. She decides that her skin looks a bit dull, and she also notices that the pimple on her nose refuses to leave.

Maybe a resurfacing mask is in order? she thinks. She takes a closer look in her magnifying mirror. She is definitely right. Her pores are clogged. This will not do. She grabs her Tata Harper organic resurfacing mask and a teddy bear foundation brush. She steadily and evenly applies the mask and grabs a magazine. She sits on her bed with her hair in a towel and reads up on the latest gossip.

"What is up with Lindsay Lohan? I can't imagine having all her opportunities and behaving like that," she says to herself. Madison, can never understand why these girls who have everything get all messed up. She continues to read as the mask hardens on her face. She checks the clock and tries to relax. Zsa is sound asleep next to her as the phone rings. Madison grabs the phone and tries to form words with her now-hardened face.

"Hello?" she manages to speak.

"Madison, is that you?" The voice on the other end does not recognize her. Her mouth is quite stiff, and she sounds muffled. Madison confirms that it is she and Mr. Donnelly identifies himself. She tries, unsuccessfully, to smile, and she explains that she has a mask on her face and that she is so sorry that she sounds funny.

Mr. Donnelly laughs and reminds her that he lives with four women. He fully understands. He first asks her how she liked the brownstone and then moves on to the job search. He is careful to keep the conversation light and assures Madison that Mr. Matthews checked in with him and he wanted to personally call her and Jade to see what the girls thought. While Mr. Donnelly is a fabulous lawyer, which, at times, makes him a great, liar, Madison knows that this is not his typical behavior. She has known Mr. Donnelly a very long time, and she smells a Kia set-up. However, she plays along. She is not mad and is actually touched that Kia has asked her dad to call, because it now gives her a less awkward way of asking him about the contract.

Madison quickly grabs a washcloth and frantically removes the facial mask. She is now able to speak clearly to Mr. Donnelly. She thanks him for all that he has done and tells him that the brownstone is completely amazing. She then begins to tell him about the job offer and the contract. Mr. Donnelly listens and then is direct and firm.

"Madison, I have an open half hour at 3:00 p.m. today. I want you to bring that contract over so we can take a good look at it."

She is relieved and very happy, and grateful for her friends. She thanks Mr. Donnelly at least three more times and then quickly hangs up and checks her time.

It is close to 12:00 noon, and she is in good shape time wise. Madison sits down at her dresser and examines the results of her mask. Her pores are visibly smaller, and she likes this. She continues with her cleanser and floral spray. She definitely needs this, and she sees the immediate benefit. Her skin is glowing and smooth, and that has her pleased. She finishes with her Tata moisturizer and continues with a quick makeup. It is a warm day so she just pulls her hair up in a messy bun, one of Madison's favorite summer styles.

Madison scans her closet and chooses the perfect little sundress. She has been dying to wear this and is excited that the warm weather is here. She tops it off with a white ultra-fine sweater and fabulous crystal hoop earrings. She is ready to take a ride to Doylestown. She again checks the time and even thinks that she might have a few extra minutes to take a stroll down Main Street before she meets with Mr. Donnelly. She considers calling Kia to thank her, but she is sure that Kia will just deny making the call to her dad. *Perhaps some things are better left unsaid?* Madison has found use of her newly discovered filter.

It is an absolutely flawless day. The sun is shining, and all of the colors of Bucks County are filling in nicely. June is always the most beautiful time for the gardeners of this area, and there are so many beautiful and scenic properties. Madison is sure that she has grown up witnessing the most perfectly manicured and decorated gardens in the world. Her eyes wander, as she is drives, and she loves the open space and beautiful farmland. She remembers the funny farm stories her dad used to tell her.

He used to say that the brown cows were the ones who produced chocolate milk. She sees those cows every day and thinks of her dad fondly. Back then she really believed that chocolate milk came from chocolate cows. She still is unsure how old she was when the actual truth was revealed. She laughs to herself now and blasts her music.

At one point in her life, she was sure she was going to be a pop star. Her very realistic and very honest mom made sure that she was aware that her gifts did not lie in her vocal chords. She remembers dance, and singing lessons, and while she wasn't a standout, she loved doing it. She constantly changes the stations, as her ADD doesn't allow for one song to finish.

Madison is close to town and looks for parking. Doylestown on a Wednesday is a tough place to park, especially for the parking impaired. She decides to park on the edge of the historic town and enjoy a nice walk. She loves downtown Doylestown and carefully scans the unique shops. There are a few antique stores that she frequents, and she can't wait to see what's new. She realizes that she has a few more minutes so she grabs a bench outside the courthouse. Mr. Donnelly's office is directly across the street.

Madison knows how precise Mr. Donnelly is and does not want to show up early. Besides the people watching is too fabulous to pass up. She watches the seriously suited lawyers bustling back and forth and tries to choose the one most in need of a makeover. She enjoys this game. Her cell phone starts to sing that familiar tune. Jade is calling, and she is in an unusually good mood. Madison can too often feel her crankiness through the airways. But, not today. She tells Madison that she received a call from the internship people and that she is needed in the city on Friday. She knows that Madison is supposed to go back for another meeting with Nina and wants to know if she can do it on Friday. She also tells Madison that she was told that Bryce Martin himself was interested in some of her construction techniques. Jade is rarely animated and she now seems ecstatic. Madison is happy for her BFF and tells her that she is on her way to a meeting with Mr. Donnelly.

She promises Jade that she will e-mail Nina after she meets with Mr. Donnelly, just in case there is an issue with the contract. They agree to talk later, and Madison is now in front of Mr. Donnelly's office.

Mrs. Clarkson greets Madison and recognizes her from the Donnelly family functions.

"Hello Madison, so nice to see you."

"Mrs. Clarkson, you are looking well and I am so happy to see you." Madison responds, feeling surprisingly grown up today.

Mrs. Clarkson dials Mr. Donnelly, and he gives her the word to send Madison right in.

Madison scurries right over to him and he stands and receives Madison with affection. She gives him a well-deserved hug. There is great love and respect between Madison and Mr. Donnelly and he has helped her tremendously for the past seven years.

Madison starts to rapidly spew. "Mr. Donnelly, thank you for helping me with this. I am just so nervous about signing a contract. It's like I am excited and scared at the same time. I don't even know all the adjectives that equate to my emotions. Anyway, I met this amazing woman. I mean, I think she is amazing. I actually met her while I was at my other interview that went so terribly." Madison takes a breath. "Did Kia tell you about any of this?"

"I have truly had a crazy week," says Mr. Donnelly.

Madison interjects that she missed him at her party. Mr. Donnelly was out of town the day Madison graduated and only Mrs. Donnelly and the girls attended. Madison continues to talk and is now speaking at a rapid rate. At this point Mr. Donnelly can't even get a word in and just waits for Madison to finish.

"Okay so I was sure that I completely lost the other job, you know the one at Faction Cosmetics. I mean the man that interviewed me I thought was just trying to steal my magazine, and of course I overreacted as usual, and I guess I really behaved in an immature manner. I mean, I think I did. I was so overwhelmed, that I am not even really sure. So anyway, I met this other woman in the bathroom at the Westin."

Madison takes another breath and makes sure she still has Mr. Donnelly with her. He is good at this, and he is still with her. He smiles and tells her to continue. She finishes the story and finally presents the contract to Mr. Donnelly and also explains that Mr. Grayson again contacted her, and she is completely confused and unsure of what to do.

Mr. Donnelly calms Madison down and assures her that he will do everything needed to check this out. He asks her to give him a day to investigate each party and to read the contract. She is so thankful and grateful and tells Mr. Donnelly how much she appreciates all that he does for her. He smiles and assures Madison that it is his great pleasure. Mrs. Clarkson now interrupts their conversation with a nervous look on her face.

"Excuse me Mr. Donnelly, those men I told you about are back." Mr. Donnelly says his goodbyes to Madison. He promises her that he will contact her tomorrow. He gives her a hug, and a kiss on the cheek, and sends her off. He then tells Mrs. Clarkson to send the men into his office.

Chapter 10

MADISON FEELS SO MUCH BETTER. She obsesses on her great fortune that is her friends and family. She checks her phone for messages and e-mails. She has a text from Jade.

Want you to come on Friday. I only have to be there for two hours and then we can check out the museums☺

And then another follows.

Tonight we are all going out to Tony's ☺

Tony's is a fabulous pizza place in Bucks County, which is known for its amazing tomato pies. The girls are obsessed with them. They just recently expanded and built a fabulous patio outside and often have new bands on

Wednesday nights. It's a fun night out for the girls and very inexpensive. Madison loves the idea. She closes her phone and decides to call Jade and do some real talking.

"Hey, my girl," Jade instantly answers. Madison tells Jade of her visit with Mr. Donnelly and then just bursts out that she can't believe that all this is happening and she is just so excited.

"It's so crazy J," she continues. "We are all really going to make it; we are all going to do something special. I just know it. I mean, you're going to intern with one of the top designers in New York. My god, aren't you freaking?" Jade laughs at Madison's drama.

"Relax, girlfriend, we have a ways to go. I'm just glad we are past the housing situation. Oh, and by the way, I handled the electric, and Kia did the other stuff. We figured you had your hands full with the job interview so we just did it. In fact, Kia is bringing a copy of the lease tonight. So, we can get everything out of the way and then her dad will do the rest."

Madison is proud of her girls. Usually, she has to nag them to get things like this done, but it seems that they are really motivated, and this is good. Madison questions the time, and they agree on 8:00 p.m. She finishes her conversation and gives Zsa Zsa a nice walk.

She pulls in the driveway and sees that her mom is home. *Maybe she will have her watch Zsa tonight?* Her baby has had a busy week, and a night home might be good for her. She walks into the kitchen and gives her mom a hug. Madison is a loving and very affectionate girl and gives hugs and kisses whenever possible. Her mom loves this attribute and often hears stories of teenagers who are just mean to their moms. She feels lucky to have such a warm, demonstrative daughter, as it is rare that they fight.

Madison is a bit schloofy, her favorite made up word for tired, and heads upstairs for a nap. She has never been much of a late-night girl, so when she knows she is going out with her friends, she tries to take a nap beforehand. They make fun of her inability to stay up late and often compare her to a little old woman. They tease her and ask "granny" if she will be able make it for a real night out. Madison admits that she is a lightweight and really needs her sleep. A fabulous night out, to her, consists of an early dinner, a movie, and then schnoogle time, of course. She does miss having a boyfriend, as that was her favorite kind of date. But right now, there is not a boy that she likes enough for that. She kicks off her shoes and slips into her bed. It takes about five minutes, and she is out.

It is now after 7 p.m., and Madison is still asleep. Her phone is ringing off the hook. She is half awake.

"Huh, uh, hello?"

"Madison! Are you still sleeping?" It is Kia, and she is now yelling at Madison to get up.

"Uh, hey K, what time is it?" Madison asks half awake.

Kia responds loudly "Uh, it is like 7:15, and we are supposed to meet at Tony's in 45 minutes. And guess what?"

Madison can barely think, let alone guess.

"Just tell me K. I am so tired."

"Gregg is bringing two of his college roommates. He met them this week and they are from the Philly area. Soooo, we are all meeting at

Tony's. Now Mads, I have never seen these guys, but I think it's time you started socializing."

Madison is still bleary, and says "K. I am getting up. I will do my best, but to tell you the truth I am so focused on this whole job and New York thing that I am just not thinking boys right now, but I will be a trooper and a good wingman."

Kia is pleased and then yells one more time for Madison to get her butt out of bed and get ready. She is coming for her at 7:45 p.m. Madison woozily agrees and hangs up.

She drags herself out of her bed and starts getting ready. She liked her outfit from today, and since she barely had it on, she decides to wear it again tonight, though a new hairstyle is definitely in order. She pulls out her Amika straightener and sections her hair. She carefully straightens each piece and uses her favorite finishing spray.

Now fully awake, she decides to amp up her makeup a bit and does her take on the smoky eye. She takes a bit of green and gold and then smokes the corners with black shadow. She then lines her eyes with lionfish smudgestick and is happy with the result. She curls her lashes and finishes with 23 strokes of Two-Timer mascara. It is hands- down her favorite mascara on the planet. She is pleased with her look and slips back into her dress.

Madison decides to change up the jewelry that she wore earlier. She goes with fun, layered bangles and long pull-through earrings. She checks her look in the full-length mirror and thinks she looks okay. She then checks the rear-view and sees the effects of the last two days of eating. She decides that she better change her dress. She looks at Zsa Zsa.

"Ugh, Zsa I look fat. I have been really eating this week. Ugh, I need to lose fifteen pounds." Zsa Zsa gives her a confused head tilt like she knows that Madison is completely insane. Madison does not have any real fat on her, but she suffers from bad body image. Her over- thinking doesn't help, and the fact that her BFF is ridiculously thin does not help either. Everyone looks fat next to Jade.

Madison settles on a cute black skirt and a pink baby doll strapless top. She changes her earrings to large pink crystal hoops. She loves these earrings, as they were a present from her mom. She is pleased with her decision to change and then spritzes herself with her favorite Pink Sugar fragrance. She grabs a preferred sweater to cover up as she is always cold and heads downstairs.

The girls have been beeping for ten minutes. Madison is late as usual. She coaxes her mom to take care of her baby, and she flies out the door.

She yells out, "Love you guys" to her mom and Zsa Zsa and tells her mom not to wait up.

Madison apologizes to her girls, but her lateness is something that they have grown accustomed to.

"No worries" they assure her in perfect sync. "We are used to you. We were listening to the new Rihanna album and just relaxing." Kia says. "I did tell Gregg that we would be there around 8:30, cause...." and Kia now gets animated, "I know my girl."

Jade and Kia playfully laugh, and they express their approval of Madison's look. "You look so pretty," Kia says. Jade agrees and adds "Not bad for just getting up." They all pass around the compliments and head over to Tony's.

Tony's is packed. The girls pull up to the valet and head to the patio. Kia immediately sees Gregg. Jade and Madison realize that by the smile on both their faces that their date must have been a success. They do a quiet yay! They are happy for Kia. The patio is full, and the band is setting up. Gregg introduces Kia and her girls to his new roommates.

"Hey girls this is John Chambers and Josh London. This is Kia, Jade, and Madison." Gregg is quite the gentleman and has already pulled the seat out for Kia. Madison and Jade watch for Kia's reaction and can tell she likes Gregg's gentleman skills. They all sit and begin to chat. There doesn't seem to be any connection between Madison and Jade with the other guys, but they seem nice enough and the girls are enjoying their company. They speak of the excitement of their individual schools and the prospect of living on their own.

The band starts playing, and while they are really good, they are also very loud. The girls have to adjust their volume for the conversation. They enjoy the music and love the pizza. The guys are really into the tomato pies, as this is something they are trying for the first time. They invite the girls to go swimming later at Gregg's. This is panic mode for Madison; she is completely nuts and insecure when it comes to putting on a bathing suit. She tries not to let her emotions show, but her girls know what she is thinking. Kia, who has real weight issues, but does not have Madison's insecurities, really wants to go. She excuses the girls for a bathroom run and wants to do some pep talking and convincing.

It is ten o'clock, and while in the bathroom, Kia is unable to convince Madison to go swimming. Madison assures her that it has nothing to do with the bathing suit issue, but that she is just tired, and, well, frankly, not into the set-up. She insists that Kia go with Gregg and then checks with Jade to see if she really wants to go. It seems that she does. Madison assures them both that she will take the car home and that the guys can drive them home. Jade kind of likes Josh. She hasn't had a date in a while, and besides, he's nice and he is tall. That is a hard combination to find. So, they all agree that Madison will excuse herself in a little while.

The girls go back to the table and talk for a while longer.

Madison likes all the guys and encourages them to be Facebook friends. She is tired and just not into the whole swimming thing, and besides she is totally preoccupied with her job. She finally excuses herself and allows the girls to continue with their fun. She gives all the guys genuine hugs and thanks them for an enjoyable evening. She also offers her share to pay, but these gentlemen will have none of it. She thanks them again and then grabs the valet ticket from Kia. She gives her a wink of approval and leaves. She does feel a bit bad for the last guy standing, but she is just not into it and heads home.

Madison arrives home at midnight and tries to be quiet, as she does not want to wake her mom. She parks Kia's car next to the mailbox and quietly slips inside her front door. She has some serious makeup removal to attend to.

She is exhausted so she does her beauty regimen quickly, but makes sure that all her mascara is off. She brushes her teeth, and then slips under the covers. She hears Zsa Zsa scratching at her mom's door and quickly pops up to release her baby. She grabs her beloved dog and schnoogles her warmly. There is nothing like kisses from Zsa Zsa, *well at least for now*. This has been a late night for Madison, and she decides it was a good time. She always loves making new friends.

Chapter 11

TODAY IS THURSDAY, AND IT is cleaning and laundry day. Madison does all the laundry in her house and the dusting. The linens need changing, and the dust just seems to procreate at night. She and her mom take turns doing the household chores, and Madison is now feeling guilty knowing that she will be leaving for New York and that all the chores will be left for her mom. She knows how hard her mother works, and she sees that age is definitely catching up to her. Her mom is turning fifty this year, and Madison wishes that her mom would meet someone to spend her extra time with. She knows that when she moves to New York, her mom is going to be very lonely, and that is very concerning to her. Even though they have a pact to meet every other weekend, it is saddens her a bit.

Madison gets up early and begins the cleaning. She hand washes all her clothing and rarely goes to the dry cleaners. She is insane about the finish on her clothing and takes much care in preserving her favorite things. Absolutely no pills are allowed. It is a major pet peeve of hers. Once a garment looks ratty, it must go into the secondhand bin. These are the things that Madison donates to Goodwill, along with outdated and outgrown clothing. Because she does not have the means to buy new things all the time, she has learned to take very good care of the possessions that she owns and loves.

Madison finishes her chores around noon and feels a surge of positive energy. She is supposed to get in touch with Nina as soon as she has a response to the contract. Madison has already written down a few questions, but truth be told, what could she ask for? She feels that from what she has read, the contract seems more than fair. She is so excited with the prospect of working with Nina and working for BLC. It almost seems too good to be true.

Madison now starts thinking about Leonard Grayson. Her stomach starts to churn a bit. She knows that she does not want to work for him, but she is so scared to make the wrong decision. She just knows it in her heart and her gut. She laughs about the whole gut thing. She is not sure where that came from, but it seems that her gut has about a ninety-four percent accuracy rate.

She even thinks about the time when she was invited to Kelly Markoff's house for a sleepover. All the middle school girls were going and Madison just felt something was wrong in her gut and did not go. That night, there was a fire at Kelly's house. No one was hurt, but from that day on, Madison, just learned to trust her gut. It is now telling her that Nina and BLC are where she should be. But she also knows that she must wait for all the information from Mr. Donnelly in order to make a sound decision. While the Grayson situation is still haunting her, she is starting to at least try to do things in an adult manner.

Madison is famous for jumping metaphorically into empty swimming pools. She gets so excited when interesting or exciting prospects come along that she sometimes says yes to things before she knows what she is getting into. Her enthusiasm is always enviable, but sometimes her decisions are amiss. Her mom is always there to quickly remind her that it is the mistakes and failures that teach us to be better and everyone knows Madison always tries to be better. This can be very difficult and many of the lessons that Madison has learned have come with hard knocks.

But, she is very sure of the BLC Concept. Her gut, her brain, and her heart, all seem to be in agreement and that does not happen often. She waits anxiously for Mr. Donnelly's call. She is now focused on Zsa Zsa, who is pacing at the door.

"Oh god, Zsa, I have been such a neglectful mommy today." With all the laundry, cleaning, and thinking, she forgot to walk Zsa Zsa and her baby hasn't been out since early this morning. Madison scoops her up and apologizes for the neglect.

"Come on, Zsa, let's go out." I will give you a proper walk around the neighborhood. I could use the exercise myself," she says to herself laughing.

Madison leashes up her girl and heads out the front door. She has been so engrossed in the house and her thoughts that she did not realize what a beautiful day it was.

The neighborhood is quiet and the lawns are very well manicured and exceptionally green. She knows that very soon the brown lawns will appear, as the summer heat takes its toll. She glances toward Mrs. Brickman's old house. She never really met the new owners. She just couldn't bring herself to go over there. She didn't mean to be rude, but she just couldn't do it. She thinks of Mrs. Brickman fondly and misses their interesting and endless conversations. Mrs. Brickman was a real patriot and loved America. She kept up on politics, Hollywood, and all the current events. Madison received a unique point of view from Mrs. Brickman and loved her very much. She knew that Mrs. Brickman was going downhill when her stories became less coherent and more repetitive.

Zsa Zsa sniffs this property intensely, and Madison can see that Zsa Zsa feels at home here. She allows her to enjoy the experience and wonders how much she remembers her former owner. Zsa Zsa loved Mrs. Brickman, and Madison is sure that she still misses her. Zsa seems satisfied and leaves her mark on her once-favorite spot. They continue down the street. Madison picks up the pace and decides to make the walk a bit more intense.

"Come on Zsa let's walk a little faster," says Madison. Zsa Zsa likes this, and they briskly walk the entire neighborhood. The two of them enjoy the time together, and their walk lasts about an hour. Madison now sees her house, and she has worked up quite a sweat. She is glad to be home. Zsa Zsa is pooped and heads right for Madison's room. Between all the cleaning and the long walk, Madison is positive that a shower is necessary. Before she gets into the shower, she checks her e-mail. She is thrilled to see one from Mr. Donnelly.

꙾   ꙾   ꙾

Hi Madison,

I read this contract thoroughly, and I must say it is a very fair offer. You have the ability to negotiate after one year, and your magazine

*will remain fully yours. The only thing that
you have to be aware of is that while you are in
the employment of BLC, you have to follow very
specific protocol. You must maintain very good
personal moral behavior and that means on and
off the job. Your contract reads that basically
you represent BLC at all times. Anyone who
knows Madison Kensington should know that
this is absolutely not an issue. Still, I outlined
a few things just to make you aware of what
they mean. I think it sounds like an amazing
opportunity. Congratulations on landing a really incredible job. I am very proud of you, and
I know that your father would be too. I am here
if you need me, but I see nothing underlying or
manipulative in this contract. I think it is a
completely fair proposition. Good luck!*

Matthew Donnelly Esquire

❧ ❧ ❧

Madison screams out loud. She is so excited
that she just can't contain herself. She knew it,
she just did. She knew the minute that she read

Nina's statement that this was her destiny. She now knows that she and Nina are going to make history. She just knows it with every fiber of her being. She is just beaming with excitement. *Oh god*, she thinks. She still has to call Leonard Grayson, however, and that is something that has her terrified. She pushes the thought from her mind and heads for the shower.

After a thorough cleansing, she slips on her favorite Betsey robe and slippers. She still wonders how this whole thing came to be. She keeps thinking about the timing at the Westin and how she nearly injured her new boss and how she must be the luckiest girl in the world. She tries to get her thoughts in order.

First she must make the call to Nina. She wants to meet with her A.S.A.P. She wants that job, and she does not want to wait another day to tell her. She decides an immediate phone call is mandatory. She checks the time and hopes that Nina will answer.

"Hello?" Nina answers on the third ring.

Madison recognizes her voice and starts to spew. "Nina, hi this is Madison Kensington, how are you?"

"Madison, it is so nice to hear your voice. I really enjoyed our time together and was hoping to hear from you."

Madison just blurts out her feelings. "I want the job you offered me. I am so excited to work for you and to be a part of BLC. I know I can do this, and I promise I will do the best job I know how."

Nina is thrilled to have Madison on her team, and they continue to discuss the plans for BLC, *Shimmer Magazine,* and a fabulous blog that Nina has already designed. Nina invites Madison to come to the city tomorrow to have lunch and discuss how they are going to move forward. Madison does not hesitate. Nina wants Madison to see the new store and wants to personally walk her through all that is evolving. They agree to meet at the store at noon.

Madison hangs up with Nina and immediately calls Jade.

"Hey, J, are you still going into the city tomorrow?" Jade is a bit more than annoyed.

"Uh…yeah… I told you I was going and that they called from my internship."

Madison hears the extra bit of attitude in Jade's voice and realizes that she has been so obsessed and consumed with herself and this job that she hasn't been the supportive friend that she should be. She profusely apologizes.

"Oh god, Jade, I have been such a bad friend. I didn't even ask you about your internship. I am so sorry I just have had complete tunnel vision and I guess I have been a little selfish. You are my best friend and I love you. I don't know what else to say."

Jade just laughs, and reminds Madison that they have been friends forever and that she knows her girl. She equates Madison's personality to that of a Ping-Pong ball trapped in a box. She knows that Madison's heart is always in the right place and she now calms down and is totally cool.

"Okay, stop apologizing, I get it," says Jade. "I know you. No worries Mads."

Madison, of course, keeps apologizing until Jade has had enough. "Just stop. I know you care. It's all good! I get it. So, what time do you want to take the train?"

Madison mentions a 9:30 a.m. train. Jade agrees, and Madison tells her that she will pick her up at 8:45.

Chapter 12

THE TRENTON STATION IS PURE insanity on a Friday, and the people-watching is as good as always. Madison and Jade are armed with their Dunkin' Donuts coffee and are taking in the peculiar sights. Madison is always fascinated when walking with Jade. Everyone swings a head or just stares at her elegance. Jade is striking and has a unique look. She is so tall and so thin and wherever she is people stare at her. Its funny how Jade is completely oblivious to this fact. Jade is completely focused on the fashion industry and in particular clothing construction.

She is an artist and a formalist and is completely intrigued with the creation of a garment. Jade is secure in her ambitions and truly wants to rule the fashion world. She walks with purpose and utter confidence, and people notice. Jade is sure that she can make fashion that no one has ever seen before. Today she has a mission. She wants to meet the man behind the Bryce Martin label. Jade will soak up all of her internship. She will watch and learn all that she needs to succeed. Jade too is a very smart and an extremely ambitious young woman.

The train ride up is quick, and Madison is unlike her normal social self on the train. She opens her laptop and spends the time organizing her thoughts and ideas. Jade sketches during the entire ride and before they know it, they are in the city. They agree to catch up after their scheduled meetings, and then they disburse. Madison decides to walk, and Jade hops into a waiting taxi. Madison heads uptown, and Jade is on her way to SoHo. Madison left Zsa Zsa home today because she felt that it might be unprofessional to bring her to a meeting with Nina. She tries not to leave Zsa Zsa often, but sometimes it is just necessary. She never even asked Nina if she liked dogs or if there was a possibility that she could bring her dog to the office with her. She decides that one thing at a time is the best way to move forward. She is pacing herself. She likes the thought and reminds herself to pace more often.

Madison walks with purpose uptown on Madison Avenue. She loves this street for obvious reasons. It is a very warm day in the city. The air is thick, and the sun is strong. She made sure to use extra sunscreen today, but she can't quite decide which of the many sunscreens that she has tried, is the best. Madison has very fair and very sensitive skin, and the one thing she vehemently believes in is good skin health.

Her favorite motto has always been "skin before makeup". She believes that the skin is like a canvas and in order for you to look your best you absolutely must care for your skin. She finds that sunscreen dries out the skin and can cause breakouts, so while she knows that it is a necessity, she tries to use it minimally on her face. She always carries a fold up large brim hat in her bag. Today, it has purpose, and she puts it on.

Madison enjoys the beautiful window displays as well as the gorgeous architectural facades and walks by a few absolutely beautiful churches. She is always in awe of older church architecture. She even signed up for an art history class that focuses on this subject. She thinks of college, and this excites her. She continues to walk and now sees Bloomingdales ahead. She knows that she is near, and her heart starts to race. As she approaches the BLC storefront, she sees that some of the paper has been taken down from the window, and she gets a peek inside.

Madison is amazed by what she sees and gets that wonderful jumpy feeling in her stomach. She see this amazing hot-pink furniture, gorgeous patterning on the walls and signage like she has never encountered. It is like a candy store for women. Madison tries the door, but it is locked, so she knocks lightly. A woman in the distance sees Madison and hurries to the door. She greets her with an engaging smile.

"You must be Madison," the young woman says. Madison smiles and is instantly taken by the warmth and grace of the young girl.

"Yes I am. So nice to meet you…uh?" The lovely young woman introduces herself as Julia Parker.

"I am the new store manager, and I have heard fabulous things about you from Nina. Welcome to our team."

Madison just reaches out and gives Julia a hug. Julia is very receptive. The girls are close in age. Julia has just three years on Madison, and with one meeting, they are sure to be great friends. Julia eagerly lets Madison know that Nina is in the back waiting for her. She directs her through the beautiful environment and shows her to the office.

Nina is immersed in a sea of boxes and papers, but is excited to see her new protégé.

"Madison, I am so happy to see you and so thrilled that we are going to have you on our team. We have so much to talk about, but first I want to show you your office." Madison thinks that she is hearing things.

"You mean I have an office, like, my own office?"

Nina laughs and welcomes Madison to the working world. She takes Madison by the hand and walks her into her new office. She also apologizes for its small stature, but assures her that if things go as she thinks that they will, Madison will soon have a much larger working space. She thanks Nina again and again and assures her that things are going to be great. She thinks but does not say that she can't believe that this little girl from Bucks County, PA has a fabulous new job in New York City, and that she is working for the smartest woman she has ever met.

Nina grabs her purse and decides that eating is the first order of business. She informs Julia where she is going and tells her that she will be back in about an hour. She tells Madison that she made a reservation at Serafina, a favorite restaurant close by. Madison is excited to hear what Nina has to say. They exit the store, and Madison has difficulty controlling her wandering eyes. She can't wait to investigate every nook and cranny of this space.

The restaurant is only a few blocks away, and since Nina is a regular, they have her table waiting. She gives Madison the skinny on the food choices, and they both end up ordering Caesar salads and decide to share angel hair pasta with lobster diablo. This is one of Nina's favorite recommendations.

Nina starts off the conversation and starts by explaining in detail the plans that she has for Madison. She wants her to write a weekly blog, and to continue writing her *Shimmer Magazine.* She suggests a few additions and tells Madison that it will have a link to the BLC website. She describes the way she wants Madison to continue connecting to her customers and adds that she has accumulated a very large list of local consumers in the area. She also tells Madison that she wants her to be the face of BLC.

Madison gets a bit sheepish about this. "The face?" she asks.

Nina laughs and tells her not to worry. She has created an animated web series and wants Madison, as the beauty and fashion editor, to share her fun and fabulous adventures as a way to connect with the customers. So, basically, she wants the animated Madison to be the icon.

Nina feels that in this capacity, Madison and BLC will rise quickly. She knows that this idea is truly unique and hopes Madison concurs.

Madison is relieved that she will be animated, as she is way too insecure to see herself on camera. That is a definite dodged bullet. The two of them continue to go over the particulars, and Madison is amazed at the creative input that is being articulated.

Nina continues to explain how she is designing web software that will also make Madison's blog and product information available to the customers in store in a very fun way. She also makes sure that Madison understands that what she writes and how she writes it is very important. She again compliments Madison on the authenticity and the genuine quality that she brings to the table. She reminds her that her truth is what will make this a success.

Their salads are delivered, and they look beautiful. Madison takes a moment to gaze around at her surroundings. She has been so focused on Nina that she hasn't absorbed the quaint setting around her. She likes the warm comfort and the authentic pizza oven in the middle of the restaurant. Madison has not eaten food today, and her lunch looks delicious. As she eats, Nina continues explaining Madison's role in her concept. Her protégé listens intensely and absorbs all of Nina's ideas.

Madison tries to process the vision that Nina has passionately articulated. She is a bit nervous, because a lot is resting on her young shoulders. Nina assures her that she is the only girl for the job and knows that she will be a great success. She then signals for the check and wants Madison to come back to the store to discuss things in more detail and to see the space and how everything will connect. Madison asks if she could pay her share of the bill. Nina smiles and appreciates Madison's offer, but this is business and it is her treat. Madison thanks Nina graciously.

The ladies exit the restaurant and head back to the store. As they walk, Nina tells Madison that she wants her to submit three blog entries twice a week. She will then meet weekly with Nina to discuss them. Nina takes out her keys, but Julia has already spotted the two ladies and quickly opens the door. Nina takes Madison on a complete tour of the amazing bi-level store. There are workmen on the second floor and Madison can see all the details that are being added. Nina shows her the fabulous spa/salon and the event and party room. There is also a café on the first floor. This is not like any store Madison has ever seen and Madison is quite the shopper. She is completely head over heels in love with BLC and her new job.

The two head into the office, and Nina gives Madison a bag of products that she considers the best in the business. She wants her to begin reviewing them, and there are many products that Madison does not recognize. Nina wants her to try them out and give her complete and honest thoughts. She also asks Madison when she can officially start her job, as there is much to do. Madison's brain is on complete overload, and her thoughts are racing. She has everything to do and does not want to say anything to disappoint Nina.

She tells her that she can start as soon as Nina needs her to, and while she has secured a place to live, she is not yet living in the city.

She quickly inserts that she can commute until then so whenever she is needed she will be available. Nina likes her spirit and gives her the option of e-mails for the next two weeks. She then explains the PR aspect of BLC and also tells Madison that she will have to make occasional live appearances. The store is not slated to open until the end of August, but they have much to do.

Madison offers to do anything to help. Her new boss assures her that she will be overloaded with work, but she will get used to the weighty schedule. Nina tells her to send her an e-mail along with the signed contract and that she will be put on the payroll next week. Then she asks if she has any concerns or questions. Madison is dazed and speechless. She assures her new employee that all is good.

"Remember, Madison, you are just doing what you have been doing for a very long time. It is just a bit more in-depth. We are going to be a great success, and you my dear, are going to be a famous celebrity."

Nina now must say good-bye to her young star. Madison hugs Nina and assures her that she is a hard worker, and she will make every attempt to be the best she possibly can be.

Madison heads outside and just as the doubting thoughts start racing through her mind, she notices a text message from Jade.

Done Yet?

Madison answers.

Just finished where r u?

Jade is in SoHo and wants to know if Madison will meet her uptown at the Whitney Museum. Madison quickly responds.

I will see you in fifteen minutes.

When she arrives, there is no sign of Jade so she sits on the steps and waits. She is thankful for her hat as the sun is really beating down on her. She takes out a notepad and jots down a few thoughts. She makes a list of to-dos and wants to move to the city as soon as possible. Jade now pulls up in a taxi, and Madison greets her.

"So how was Bryce Martin?" She makes sure that she does not just dump all of her thoughts on Jade and shows genuine interest in Jade's experience. Jade, being Jade, was a bit cynical about her new boss and thought that he was a bit artificial. Nevertheless she felt that she got some needed experience and knows that she needs to keep her comments to herself. It is the connections that will help her achieve her goals, and Jade is smart enough to know when to keep quiet. She has a filter and always uses it. Jade now focuses on Madison.

"So give me the details. How was your lunch meeting?" Madison starts speaking rapidly.

"Jade I can't even tell you how excited I am. I am so lucky. Nina is amazing, the store is amazing and the concept, well, the concept is like nothing I have ever seen out there. I am so overwhelmed and nervous and thrilled and..." Jade now has to slow Madison down.

"Mads, didn't I tell you, you have got to pace yourself. Damn girl, you're going to give yourself a heart attack. Speak slower. I can't even understand what you're saying." Jade puts her arm around Madison and suggests a seat on the steps.

"Okay, now tell me what this job really entails," Jade says calmly.

Madison slows her thoughts and tells Jade all that transpired. Jade is happy for her girl and reminds her in her sarcastic manner to not forget the little people when she is a famous cartoon. They both laugh, and in perfect sync say,

"From your mouth to god's ears." Jade makes a few more jokes, and then they enter the Whitney. The girls clear their minds and enjoy the exhibits.

Chapter 13

BACK IN BUCKS COUNTY, KIA has been called home for an emergency. She has been out all day with her mom getting the things she needs for her new living space. They got an urgent call from Mr. Donnelly, and he needs to have a family meeting at home. This has never happened before, and Kia and her mom are worried. They drop everything and rush home.

Madison and Jade have thoroughly examined the beautiful exhibits at the Whitney and are exhausted and ready to leave. It is now five o'clock, and they consider their options. Should they deal with rush hour or stay and have dinner in the city? Madison really wants to get home.

She wants to start to organize and get ready for the move. She easily convinces Jade and they grab a taxi to Penn Station.

Kia and her mom pull into the driveway. Kia's home is a beautiful single family home and quite grand. They see that Mr. Donnelly's car is already there, and they burst through the door with concern. Kia's younger sisters are still at their afterschool studies, and Mr. Donnelly is sitting alone in the living room. Kia immediately rushes over to her father and throws her arms around him.

"Daddy, is everything okay? Are you all right? I am so worried."

"What's all this about?" Mrs. Donnelly says as she sits down next to her husband. She thinks she knows. "Does this have anything to do with the FBI visiting your office?"

Mr. Donnelly is caught completely off guard. "How did you know that?"

" Well, I called your office the other day, and Mrs. Clarkson told me you were in a meeting. She used the word agents and I got concerned and pressed her to tell me what was going on. She said she had no idea why the FBI would be here and she thought that maybe they were investigating one of your clients. It sounded strange to me, and when you didn't tell me I started to worry. "Matthew," Mrs. Donnelly continues, "you always tell me everything. What the hell is going on?"

Mr. Donnelly starts at the beginning. "I had no idea that one of my clients was laundering money. I really didn't. I was doing some legal work for him and I guess I didn't ask the right questions. I screwed up big time. I really do not know where this is going to go, but I wanted to prepare my family for the worst."

Kia is silent and the tears just start rolling down her cheeks. This is her dad, her idol. He is perfect. He can't be a criminal. This isn't possible. She runs out of the room, hysterical, and heads for her car. She just can't look at her dad right now. Everything she thought, everything she believed and knew was wrong. Kia is crushed. She just sits in her car and cries. She then dials her girls. She needs them and she needs them now.

It is now close to seven and the girls are back at Trenton Station. They go right to the car and head home. Madison checks her phone and sees two missed calls from Kia. She calls her back.

"Hey, K, what's up?" Madison hears Kia's voice and is immediately worried. Kia just asks her to bring Jade and meet her at Madison's A.S.A.P. Kia, does not even want to be home and Madison's house is the best place she can think of right now. Madison presses her.

"Kia, what is wrong? You sound horrible. Oh my god, we are coming."

Kia just hangs up and keeps crying. She starts the car and heads to Madison's. Her perfect life and her perfect father are all a lie. Kia is falling to pieces. She was always taught to do the right thing. Her parents, especially her dad, always instilled in her the concept of being honest. Kia is confused, upset, and so angry. Why would her dad need to do this? She tries to make sense of it.

He is so smart and so successful. They have everything. *How could this be true?* She now considers that maybe it isn't true. Maybe there is a real explanation and that maybe her dad is innocent. She doesn't know what to think.

Kia pulls into Madison's driveway and nervously waits for her two best friends. She sits in silence. It takes about twelve minutes until the girls pull up. They see Kia's car and rush to her. Madison opens the car door to find Kia looking almost catatonic.

"K, what is going on? What happened?" Madison slides in next to her and guides Kia out of the car. Jade studies her and thinks she is in shock. Kia has still not said a word. Jade shakes her.

"K, what the hell is going on?

Kia's eyes start to well up again, and the girls see that she has been crying.

"K, talk to us. You can say anything, we will understand. How can we help you?" Madison says.

The girls lead Kia inside the house and sit her down. Kia slowly starts to speak. Her voice is shaky and her words are a bit incoherent. She tells the girls all that she knows right now, and how she ran out of her house as fast as she could. She said that she felt like she was choking and she just couldn't breathe. Madison and Jade both comfort her and tell her that they are sure that it must be some kind of mistake. They assure Kia that her dad is a very good man. Kia wants to believe that they are right. She does believe that there is more to this story and feels so sick that she really can't breathe. As she continues to talk, she feels herself becoming woozy. Kia now turns paste white, and considering her dark complexion, Jade and Madison think that they should get her to the hospital. They go into panic mode and start to guide Kia toward the living room sofa.

Before they can take a step, Kia passes out right in Madison's kitchen. Madison and Jade are about to call 911 when Madison's mom walks in. The girls are holding Kia, and Madison's mom goes into action. She grabs smelling salts and gently holds Kia up. She and the girls make sure that Kia is now safe in a kitchen chair, and they each hold her side. Madison's mom also applies a cool washrag on her forehead and gently strokes Kia's face.

"Kia, are you with me?" She tells Madison to get Kia some water while she holds her head up. Kia is now slowly coming back, and she is coherent. "What happened?" she asks.

"Honey, you passed out. From what the girls have told me I think you hyperventilated and caused yourself so much anxiety that you just went down. I need you to relax and calm down. I checked your pulse and am sure you will be fine. You gave us a bit of a scare."

Madison's mom is calm and strong, and Kia feels safe. She wants to get up and go to the sofa. The girls fill Mrs. Kensington in on the situation, and she offers comfort to Kia.

"Listen sweetheart, whatever has happened I have known your parents for a very long time, and no matter what, you have to be supportive and respectful of your father," says Mrs. Kensington. If you let me, I would like to take you home. I think you need to talk all this out with you parents."

Madison watches in awe at the strength of her mom. She is so kind and loving. She convinces Kia to go home with her and talk this out with her parents. She also reminds Kia of something that Madison has also had to learn recently. "Things are not always as simple as right and wrong, or black and white. This is a fact of life, and things sometimes can get complicated."

Madison's mom wants Kia to first call her parents and let them know that she is okay and then she comes up with a fabulous idea. She is sure that Kia is fine and thinks that a good meal will bring up Kia's blood sugar and also change the tone of the situation. She knows that Kia is fine, just visibly shaken, and she also knows that none of them have eaten. So dinner with friends and family comes first, and then she can face her father. This seems like a good solution. Kia says that she is not hungry but agrees to the idea.

She can't believe that she passed out. She feels embarrassed. Madison's mom assures her that she was probably in panic mode, and the heavy breathing made her faint. Madison quickly realizes that in all the commotion she never let Zsa Zsa out. Her poor baby has been in her room all day. Madison quickly runs upstairs and frees her baby. She runs her outside and her angel pees and poops.

The girls agree to dinner, and Italian sounds perfect. Madison runs and gets Zsa Zsa's bejeweled bag and assures her girl that she is going with them. She promises scraps for her and Zsa Zsa jumps right into the bag. La Stalla is close by, and the food is fabulous. Kia sits for a few more minutes and then stands and is ready to go.

Madison's mom calls the Donnellys herself and assures them that Kia is safe and that she will bring her and her car home after dinner. The tone at dinner is changed by the positive attitude of Kia's BFFs. She now knows that they are with her no matter what. She is feeling a bit better. The girls tell Kia of their experiences of the day and eat delicious food. They convince Kia to eat her favorite pasta dish and for the moment all is well.

Jade drives Kia's car and follows Mrs. Kensington to the Donnelly's. They all get out of the car and walk Kia to the door. Kia hugs her girls and then turns to Madison's mom and thanks her for everything. Madison's mom promises Kia that everything will be okay and if she needs anything to call her. Both the Donnellys open the door and are relieved to see Kia. They thank Mrs. Kensington and agree to speak later. Jade and Madison drive home with Madison's mom and speak nothing more of the situation. It is a quiet ride home.

Madison asks Jade to spend the night, as it has been a while since they had a sleepover. Madison decides that she will give Jade and herself a facial and they will just hang out and have a stress-free girl's night. Jade loves the notion and is game for anything. Definitely a light movie is in order. They go inside and head for Madison's room. Madison stops and thanks her mom for, well, just being her mom. She hugs and kisses her and tells her that she loves her. That means everything to Madison's mom.

Jade and Madison feel horrible about what just transpired and decide not to talk about it for the rest of the night. Madison takes a quick shower while Jade considers the movie choices. "Ten Things I Hate About You" seems perfect. Madison comes out of the bathroom quickly and is just so happy to be clean from the New York grit. She turns over the bathroom to Jade, who, too is quickly in and out. Madison loves the movie choice and then paints a resurfacing mask on Jade's face and her own. They decide to make some popcorn and they splurge and do the pay per view on the big flat screen downstairs.

They grab some extra comfy blankets and start the movie. They sit quietly as their faces harden from the facial mask. They both love this movie. About halfway through the movie, Madison pauses it and gives Jade a hot towel to remove her mask. Madison examines the results and is pleased. Jade checks the mirror and agrees. Madison now removes her mask and sprays her face and Jade's with her favorite floral hydrating spray. She and Jade finish with the nutrient complex vitamin roller ball and then continue the movie. Their skin feels amazing and the aromatherapy that is in these products really gives them a lift.

For Jade and Madison, this movie has had several viewings. The Julia Styles character is one that they both relate to. After the credits roll, the girls focus their thoughts on Kia. They wonder how she is doing and decide to send her a text. Madison takes out her phone and texts *Love you, M and J.*

Today is Saturday, and Madison and her two BFFs have had a heck of a week. Madison gets up early and is careful not to wake Jade. She scoops up Zsa Zsa and takes her outside. The day is hot and muggy. Madison sits at her favorite childhood picnic table in her yard. She watches as Zsa Zsa plays in the tall grass and considers her week. She tries to grasp all that has happened. She equates this week to an emotional rollercoaster and can't even understand all that she is feeling. Her mind is full of questions.

She wonders what she can do to help her friend. Madison does not even want to consider that Mr. Donnelly might be guilty of a crime. She knows that this will just crush Kia. She also wonders how all of this will affect the move to New York. Madison somehow feels that the girls should rethink the living arrangements. The whole situation is overwhelming and uncomfortable. She wonders if she should even bring this up, or if she should just keep her thoughts to herself.

Jade is now awake and walks down to the kitchen. She sees Madison outside and walks up behind her. She sits down next to her friend and asks, "What's up?"

Madison is deep in thought and turns to Jade. "I was just thinking about this whole week. It has just been crazy. I am so upset for Kia. It is just so unbelievable. I am sitting here thinking what we should do. I am completely lost for an answer."

Jade is a true realist. She is also finite in her opinion.

"Look Mads, we can only be here for Kia. This is her personal business, and we need to stay out of it. We also need to treat her like we always do. I think that this is really important. We can't change how we look at her in the face of things. She is our best friend, and the worst thing we can do is make her even more self-conscious."

Madison is not sure if she agrees with Jade. In fact she is not sure of anything. She does know that she now has a job and it is time to focus on this fact. Madison has found her answer. She must delve into her responsibility. She and Jade walk back into the kitchen, and Madison takes out the Honey Bunches of Oats. She pours two bowls, and she and Jade eat silently.

Jade also has much to do and gathers her things. Madison realizes that Jade does not have her car and quickly throws on her clothes and drives Jade to her home. They say their good-byes and agree to talk later. Madison hurries home and is ready to get down to her work. She considers her future and focuses on her mission. Madison knows that she is in charge of her own destiny and she must keep her promise to herself and continue on her path. She returns home and is now ready to get down to some serious work. She first checks her e-mail. There are many messages waiting.

Nina is in her office very early today as she has some serious deadlines to reach. She tries to take Saturdays off, but there is just no time left, and the opening of BLC cannot wait. Nina has set the opening for September 1, and September is approaching quickly. Nina wants to get the BLC blog up and running and is thrilled that Madison is going to work for her. She composes a, to-do list for Madison and sends her the template for the blog.

Nina has organized a schedule and wants Madison to be prepared for a media blitz. Nina has hired a major New York public relations firm, and has big plans for Madison K. and BLC. She has also hired another young woman named Angela Martin to assist her with her daily tasks. Angela was raised on the tough streets of Harlem and has, in spite of a very difficult personal history, managed to graduate community college. Angela has toughness and a spirit that Nina likes, and she thinks that Angela will make a valuable contribution to the team. Nina has a strong feeling that BLC is going to rise quickly. Even Nina has no idea what is about to happen.

Madison's Bedroom

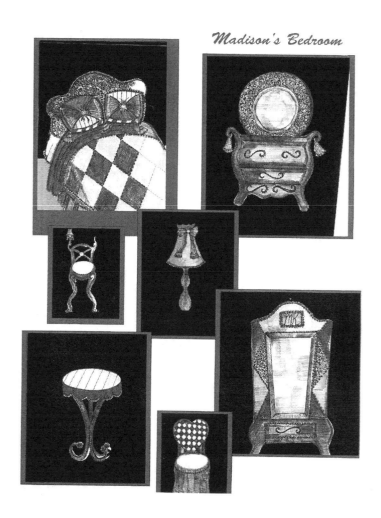

Madison K.

Madison's Favorite Vintage

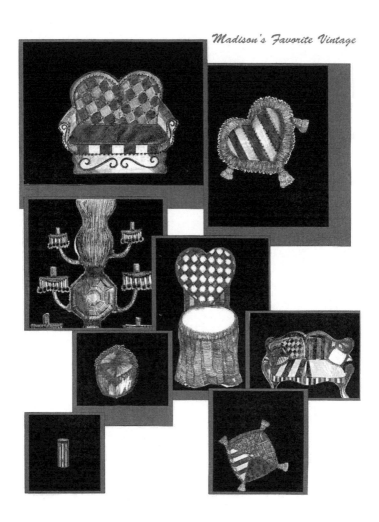

189

Madison K.

Madison's
Handbag
Collection

Café
Cuisines

Madison Vintage
Frames

What If
A Personal Statement
by Nina Hagen

*W*HAT IF WE SAID WHAT we meant and we meant what we said? What if we could make money based on the truth and a core of integrity? What if we sold products that we believed to be the best and promoted them as such? What if we were in control of the celebrity status by building our celebrity based on genuine and personal facts? What if we had an original thought; not one copied or created out of manipulation and angles?

A good idea and a creative thought must come from a core of integrity or it is basically a lie. As an artist I strive to represent truths based on facts and honesty. At the end of the day if we mean it, we will succeed. Sound too good to be true? Well that is the point. We have so gotten used to believing that we have to lie, cheat, or steal in order to succeed when the answer is really simple.

Be great at what you do. Always try to be better. Never think you are finished and learn from everything. This is my Jerry Maguire moment. This is my creative and artistic vision based on experience, humanity, and genuine knowledge. I am tired of being surrounded by mediocrity based on corporate manipulation.

Retail is a disaster, and the customers are confused. Television is an array of voyeuristic dramas that equate gossip and hate to a new level. We, as a creative society, have sunk to an all-time low. I believe that we can be better - better in every aspect of our creative lives. What if we created an entire industry without exploitation derived from creative ideas evolved in a genuine manner?

This concept encapsulates all of the above. BLC is the future of the beauty and entertainment industry. With every fiber of my being I know this to be true. While technology continues to soar, humanity continues to nose-dive. We have no talent celebrities pushing products that they don't even use, and magazines and publications giving precedent to products in a biased methodical way. Where is all the talent? I will tell you that it is being squashed by corporate egos and fear.

Every large brand in this country was created by an individual or individuals, but as corporate giants continue to consume these brands, the creativity in business continues to disappear. They are milking the proverbial cows to death. We need to reevaluate where this path leads. I believe that we are seeing first hand, through our current economy and social disarray, where this leads.

While my focus is on creative retail and entertainment, I believe there is an underlying metaphor for humanity. Now this is quite a large area to cover, but there are things that I have witnessed and they all seem to come down to control. This is control across the board. The powers that be want and are controlling every aspect of our lives and will continue to do so until the general public wakes up. We are, in this great country, supposed to be free citizens; free to create, free to achieve, and free to fail. What if that was really the case? What if freedom was in the confines of a metaphoric box? What if the boundaries were set in place for corporate giants who only wanted to protect their own interests?

Now you may ask yourself, what any of this has to do with a retail beauty concept? In fact I would say that may be fair. What if this scenario is applicable to all the current venues in our country? I believe in fair business practices. But what if the majority of the products were owned by one or two large companies, and they colluded with the media and the publications, and the only agenda was destroying the little guy and controlling the masses, the only real competition. The truth is that they either buy their competition or destroy them.

This concept is one with legs. It is an entire story, an entire entity that will succeed based on the foundation. What if we were not for sale? What if we worked to earn the customer based on humanity? What if we said what we meant and we meant what we said? Hmmm that might be refreshing. We are the little guy - the guy that designed, engineered, and created what they represent. What if the media was not reporting the facts, but reporting what the giants were paying them to report? Hmmmm.. Now apply this theory to medicine, war, and politics. Scary huh.

I believe that all people are sick of being lied to and falsely promised. This is not just a concept, but this is the real way to do business. There is a crack in the foundation of corporate America, and now is the time to move. The paradigm is shifting, and the sleeping giant is awake. BLC and all of its ideas are ripe for change in the way America does business.

About the Author and Editor

NINA KAPLAN, THE AUTHOR OF *Madison K. Live, Life, Fun,* grew up in the beauty and retail businesses learning the tricks of the trade at a young age. She followed her passion for art and all things beautiful while studying at Tyler School of Art and Yale Graduate School for Fine Arts. Eventually Kaplan created and ran several successful women's clothing, jewelry and home design stores for two decades. It was her time spent in these stores where Kaplan watched her loyal customers connect with the exquisite in-store items, the dedicated staff and with each other.

One such customer was Rachel Levy Lesser, who shopped along with her mother and aunt, in Kaplan's stores since she was a little girl. Rachel grew up, graduated from The University of Pennsylvania and The University of Michigan Business School, and went on to write a successful book about shopping in Kaplan's stores.

At the same time, Nina became more interested in these unique connections women and girls made through their shopping experiences, and she also watched as her own young daughter, Madison, searched for a role model that she could relate to and believe in.

It all came together in 2010 when Nina launched BLC (Beautylandcouture,) the latest and most unique concept in the beauty business today. Kaplan only carries products at BLC that she believes in, and to demonstrate that these products truly work, she created BLC's animated Fashion and Beauty Editor, Madison K. Madison is a true combination of Nina, Nina's now 19 year-old daughter, Madison, and she represents a little bit of the girl in every woman.

Madison K. grew into a unique personality at BLC reviewing products for the BLC Blog, picking her own in-store "Madison's Favorites" and writing the quarterly in-store *Shimmer Magazine*. Nina knew there was a bigger story to tell, and she did just that by writing *Madison K. Live, Life, Fun* – the first installment in the Madison K. book series. She called upon her loyal customer, Rachel, to help her edit the book, and since then, Madison K. has been going strong!

Remember as Madison K. always says...
.."It's all about the fun!"

XOXXO,
NINA & RACHEL

Made in the USA
Charleston, SC
06 November 2011